Coming Out

First Edition, 2017

ISBN: 9781547151936

Jay Argent
jay@jayargent.com

www.jayargent.com

Coming Out

Jay Argent

One Day at a Time (Charlie's Story)

The absolute worst room in the entire school—worse than the bio lab during frog dissection season, when the whole room smells like formaldehyde, and worse than the basement bathroom that the janitor never cleans and is always sticky and smells like cigarette smoke—is the locker room.

Every other day, before and after track practice, I have to deal with a room full of loud, sweaty teenage boys getting undressed. I take a deep breath before going through the door, ready to rip my uniform off and put my school clothes back on as quickly as humanly possible, saying to myself the whole time, *Just keep your head down, don't look at anyone, head down, don't look, c'mon.*

The whole place is steamy from the showers, the tiled floors slippery and the walls dripping with condensation. Metal lockers slam open and shut, towels get whipped around, reeking shoes get shoved in duffel bags.

Look down, I keep telling myself as Jake and Simon, whose lockers are right next to mine, laugh and joke with each other about who ran the fastest, who's going to win the match next week. Out of the corner of my eye, I know they're taking their shirts and shorts off. *Look down and hurry up.*

It's not that I'm attracted to Jake and Simon (I mean, they're good-looking, but they're assholes), but it's that I'm afraid that if I look directly at them, or at any of my teammates while they're half-naked, they'll *know*, I mean, they'll see right through me. It won't be that I'm just looking at them to have a conversation, to make a joke, or to ask about a history assignment. They'll think I'm looking at them because I want them, because I think they're hot, because I want to see them naked or kiss them or whatever it is they imagine gay guys think about all day. Like we can't just talk to another guy without it being *weird*.

If I look at them, I'm convinced that they'll know I'm gay, that they'll see it in my eyes. I can't let them know. No one can know. Ever.

"Hey Charlie, what's the rush?" I hear Danny ask from behind me. He says this after every practice. I'm just pulling my shorts down, and can feel my cheeks flush.

"I've got a ton of homework to start," I mumble, not turning around. "Gotta get home."

"Teacher's pet over here," Jake shouts.

"Gotta keep that 4.0," I try to joke. My foot gets caught in my jean leg, and they won't tug on. *Damn it, c'mon, c'mon.* My heartbeat quickens.

I flick my eyes over to Simon and Jake, both with towels wrapped around their waists, getting into an argument about who has the worst grades in calculus. Jake pokes Simon in the chest, and Simon retaliates by trying to rip Jake's towel off him, but Jake keeps a firm grip on it.

"Hey, get off me, fag!" Jake shouts at Simon, and they both head toward the showers, still arguing. Thank God the stalls are private and curtained. But still, I refuse to shower here. I always wait until I get home.

That word, "fag," gets tossed around a lot in the locker room, and in the school halls, and in the cafeteria. Every time I hear it I can feel myself retreating into myself a bit more, like a hedgehog bundling itself up into a ball.

Of course, my shirt is inside-out. That's another five seconds I'll have to spend in here. While I sit down and try to reverse it, I feel a hand against the skin of my back.

"Hey, Charlie," a voice I recognize says. "You made awesome time today." I slip my arms through my shirt, but don't tug it over my head yet. At least I can cover up my scrawny, pale chest. I'm always embarrassed by my body. Why aren't I getting bigger, more muscular, like the rest of the guys?

I glance up and see Ray looking down at me. He's showered and dressed already, bag slung over his shoulder. His jet-black hair is still wet, and falls in thick strands over his deep brown eyes. He has a warm smile on his face, and a few drops of water slide down his cheeks. His skin is the color of coffee with a hefty pour of cream in it. I have the sudden urge to reach my hand out and wipe the water from his cheek, brush his hair out of his eyes. *Shit*, I think, *shit, I'm looking at him, he knows, he knows.* "Thanks, Ray," I say, turning around. I pull my head through my shirt, grab my bag, and get ready to sprint out of there. I head for the door, rushing past Ray.

"Hey, you wanna go for a run Satur—" I hear Ray say to me as I leave. But I'm already gone, power-walking down the hall, out the door, into the bright afternoon sun.

Walking up the grassy hill toward the train tracks and the shortcut home, I realize I left my binder in my locker. My binder with all of my English notes and homework. I look in my backpack to see if I at least remembered my copy of *Hamlet*. Nope.

But I can't go back. I can get to school early tomorrow, grab my binder and book and finish my homework in record time, before the first bell even rings.

No turning around. I sigh, and keep walking.

I really hate the locker room.

Chapter 2

That this too too solid flesh would melt,
Thaw, and resolve itself into a...into a...a puddle?

Ugh, no. We have to memorize a Shakespearean monologue by Monday for Mr. Mack's English class, and of course I chose one of the hardest. Hamlet being all melodramatic. And with my copy of the play back in my locker, I just have some crappy Internet edition without any footnotes to explain what the hell I'm actually saying.

I'm pacing my room, trying to recite this thing from memory. There's not much room to pace. Mom and I live in a two-bedroom split-level that's so old we can always tell where the other is by the particular sound of each creak. *Crrr-eak.* Mom's in the living room, about to flip the TV on. *Cr-ee-ee-ee-eak.* That's me walking down the hallway at 3:00 a.m. for a snack. Absolutely no privacy, not even with the doors closed.

I can hear the sizzle and smell the onion-y odor of the Hamburger Helper that Mom's cooking. We're a family—if you could call two people a family—of dinners that come out of cardboard boxes. Mom's too exhausted after coming home from work to make much else. Weekends we either order pizza or go out, usually to the Chinese buffet or the Indian buffet—really, any buffet will do—in the strip mall along the highway. For anything fancier, we'd have to drive the half-hour to Johnstown, which isn't exactly bursting at the seams with Michelin-rated establishments.

We've moved between a few different Pennsylvanian towns in my life. The first move was to get away from Dad, a perpetual drunk and professional collector of unemployment. Mom served him with divorce papers, we packed up, and rented an apartment outside of Erie for a few years. We got to spend every summer weekend at the lake, but winters were awful—cold, gray, and wet.

Now we're surrounded by hills and forests, beautiful in the summer and fall, but just different shades of brown any other time. It used to be a mining town, but that industry disappeared when the coal did, along with most of the people. Now, it's mostly car part manufacturing and home restoration contractors for the huge McMansions up in the mountains.

How weary, stale, flat, and...unpromisable...

Looks to me...every...purpose of the world?

I give up and flop down on my bed. The ancient mattress, dragged from home to home over the past decade, squeals in pain.

"Charlie!" Mom shouts, though really she could whisper and I'd hear her. "Don't you lie on that bed in your dirty clothes! I just washed the sheets!" Of course she could hear the mattress, too. I get up quickly, making sure the mattress squeaks again, then wait ten seconds before lying back down very slowly so it doesn't make a sound.

My eyes drift closed, and I suddenly feel deeply exhausted. Between school and practice and homework...not to mention the whole locker room thing, which has been playing over and over in my mind since I got home…

In my half-dreaming state, I see Ray's face. That half-smile he always has on. His perfectly effortless "I woke up like this" sense of style. His broad shoulders and the nape of his neck that I stare at all through English class, curls of dark hair just drifting over it. How, sitting behind him, I can catch the scent of his shampoo. How when he turns around to pass back a stack of papers, our fingers sometimes graze each other's as I take them, and how sometimes he looks right at me, and I forget to pass back the rest until Amanda whacks me on the back with her pencil. How I want to bend forward and bury my face in his hair, take in his smell, run my lips against his neck—

"Charlie, dinner!" Mom yells, and I jump awake. The bed squeaks, and I cringe, but she's too busy clattering around with the dishes and silverware to hear it.

My pants have gotten tighter since I laid down, and I realize that all my fantasizing over Ray has affected more than just my head. I always feel so ashamed when this happens—disgusted, even. What am I doing? Why can't I fantasize about Megan Fox or whatever celebrity Simon and Jake are drooling over this week?

Quickly, I turn my thoughts back to the monologue:

Fie on it! Oh, fie! Tis a garden...untended?

That grows to seed...

Try as I might, I still can't get the damn thing right. But at least I can eat dinner now without it looking like there's a relay baton in my pants.

Nothing like Shakespeare to kill a boner.

After dinner, I get a text from Amanda:

hey asshole, wanna go 2 homecoming?

I alternate between being really amused and really confused. Amanda's been my closest friend since freshman year. We both went to middle school in different towns, so didn't know anyone when we started at Carlisle High. She came into homeroom on our first day with bubblegum-pink hair and a shirt that had "WOMEN'S RIGHTS ARE HUMAN RIGHTS" written on it in big letters. Everyone but us two seemed to have known each other since birth, joking around and catching up on what they did over summer break. I just slouched in my chair. She sat in the desk next to mine, and as we listened to the other kids' inane conversations about skinny dipping and wine coolers, waiting for the announcements to start—the universal sign for everyone to shut up—she turned to me and said, "Did you know that the loose skin covering your elbow is called a 'weenus'?"

So that's how Amanda and I became friends.

Nobody knows what color Amanda's hair actually is—I'm pretty sure even Amanda doesn't remember—but as of yesterday it was a psychedelic combination of the electric blue she had colored it last month with streaks of fire-engine red, bleeding together into purple. I'm amazed that in the three years I've known her, she's managed to change colors so frequently without her hair falling out from all the chemicals. You wouldn't know it by looking at her, but Amanda's parents are loaded.

Our school is on the border of where the poor folks like Mom and I live and the twenty-bedroom palaces up in the mountains. Both sides of town are small enough for all the kids to go to one school.

Amanda's dad does something involving hedge funds that neither of us understands, and her mom is a yoga instructor who charges hundreds of dollars an hour with private clients. Amanda always jokes that she's pretty sure her mother is actually a high-end hooker. Her brother is a junior at Princeton, with perfects grades and a straight track into law school. But Amanda, well, she gets good grades, but otherwise, she's the complete opposite of what her parents imagine a perfect daughter should be. She drives a 1960s VW Beetle, paints murals with her fingers, is the drummer for an all-girl pop-punk garage band called Beatup Bitches, and plans on going to art school.

afterparty @ ur place? I text back.

Despite their cavernous home with a heated swimming pool, and the frequency with which her parents leave her alone in the house while they take couples' cruises to the Maldives, Amanda's never held a rager. She prefers sneaking her parents' liquor over to the playground after dark so she and I can get mildly buzzed while complaining about college applications.

only if u bring the whole team, she texts back.

Amanda loves to joke with me about watching the track team practice and salivating over everyone running around in those tiny shorts. She's only kidding in her usual obnoxious way, but it makes me uncomfortable. I could never tell her why, though.

why don't u ask danny? I text her.

She acts like she doesn't have a huge crush on Danny from the team, but she always talks about him when we drink her dad's Johnny Walker.

fuck you dickhole pops up on my phone, a not uncommon phrase coming from Amanda.

why do u even want to go? I ask her.

because i wanna see u all dressed up in a suit, she writes, followed by, *and i've always wanted an excuse to wear that quincenera dress i found in the dumpster.*

Amanda's not the type to go to school functions. She always swears that she'll "Go all Carrie on everyone" if she's ever forced to go to prom.

u srsly wanna go? I ask.

i've been asked to go, she finally admits.

HAHAHA!! I send back. *WHO???*

fuck you dickhole, and it's sean costa. Sean Costa is the six-and-a-half-foot tall redheaded president of the drama club.

and you said yes??? I ask.

i felt bad for the gangly dickhole, she writes. Amanda does have her soft side. *i was surprised, tho*, she writes again, *i always thought he was gay.*

My heart sinks. I don't want to hear this coming from her. I've never discussed my feelings with anyone, not even Amanda. I even make up crushes on girls in school, just to keep up appearances. One time, when we were both pretty drunk, Amanda and I even kissed. We both agreed it was one of the worst experiences of our mutual lives and still joke about it.

Nobody's gay in our school—at least, no one's *out*. This isn't exactly the most forward-thinking part of the country. Our sex-ed program is abstinence-only, and churches are packed on Sundays. I can't even imagine the kind of humiliation I'd go through if anyone found out I was gay. You hear about kids around the country getting bullied, beat up, even killing themselves because of their sexuality. I couldn't face that. I'm not strong enough to fight everyone off. I just want to keep my head down, ignore it, and move the hell out of this town.

But the truth is, I don't know if, even once I'm in college, I'll ever be able to really be myself. I hate this part of me. If I could get rid of it, I would. If I could magically become straight, I'd do it in a heartbeat. I'd give *anything* to find boobs hot. To be like any other guy. To be able to relax in the locker room, for once.

One night, when I was a kid, my dad was six or seven beers gone and watching the news. One of the states had voted to legalize same-sex marriage. This apparently lit a fuse, and my dad exploded. He started screaming about the "homos," how filthy and disgusting they are, how they're all going to hell and deserve to be lined up and shot. How he'd punch the shit out someone if he ever found out they were gay.

Then he turned to me and said, "You stay away from them, Charlie! They'll touch you, they'll kidnap you and torture you!" He went on and on like this until my mother started yelling back at him to shut up, then things just devolved into the usual nightly shouting match.

so???? Amanda texts. I realize I hadn't responded to her last message.

ok, I type back.

u need to bring someone, she writes.

i'll figure it out, I say. *gotta go.*

I set my alarm for well before sunrise. I need to get my English stuff from the locker room and finish that homework before the first bell rings in the morning.

i always thought he was gay keeps running through my head. Does Amanda think *I'm* gay? Do I *act* gay? Do I *sound* gay? Do I *dress* gay? What does Sean do that made Amanda think *he's* gay? Do *I* do any of that?

I lay awake, my thoughts racing, until well after midnight. Finally, I decide to try and work on that monologue again, in my head.

Heaven and earth….An increase of appetite…
Growing by what it feeds on...Let me not think of it…
Frailty, thy name is woman!

Nothing like Shakespeare to put you to sleep.

Chapter 3

There's an old set of train tracks that runs through the stretch of woods between my neighborhood and school. If you follow them, it cuts a good ten minutes off the walk to and from school, quicker than walking down Bower's Run Road, around Chestnut Hill, and through Clarke Park and the playground.

The tracks are overgrown, probably haven't been used for at least fifty years. Because the rail ties are covered with dirt and grass, it also makes a great running path. The trees that line either side of the tracks hang over them, forming a kind of tunnel. This morning, with the sun just rising and bathing the red, orange, and yellow autumn leaves in its glow, it's really beautiful.

It's hard to appreciate the beauty right now, though, given that I've gotten about four hours of sleep, haven't had breakfast, and am in a rush to finish my homework.

There's a door in the back of the school that's supposed to be an emergency exit and kept locked from the outside. Everyone knows, though, that if you jiggle the handle in just the right way, you can open it and get inside. The door opens right into the pool, or what used to be the pool, now empty and unused. Carlisle High hasn't had a swim team since the school board cut the district's budget a few years back. Stoners tend to sneak in after hours and smoke in the empty pool. Rumor has it that Frank, the school janitor, sells weed to students.

After some strategic wiggling and pulling, I manage to open the door and slip inside. I walk around the cavernous pool, still smelling like stale chlorine, around to the door to the locker room, where I flick on the fluorescent lights. Frank's made some vague attempt to clean up, but lockers still hang open, socks dangling from them, and muddy cleats from the soccer team are still scattered on the floor. No amount of effort can get rid of the stench of sweat and body odor. I walk over to my locker, and my mouth drops open.

Empty.

Shit. Shit shit shit.

Who the hell took my stuff? Frank? Jake or Simon, just to screw with me? I sit down on a bench, defeated. Well, looks like I'll be arriving to Mr. Mack's class sans homework after all. Hopeful, I check all the lockers around mine. Nope, nothing but dirty shirts and the odd tennis ball. I check the lockers in the other row, too. Nada.

Then, I open the last locker. This one smells different. Clean. Familiar. There's a rumpled black shirt hanging on the hook inside.

Then I realize what it smells like. It smells like Ray.

I stand there, paralyzed. The urge to reach in is overwhelming. I know it would be wrong, that it would violate his privacy. But no one's here. If I took his shirt out, just to touch it, just to feel it, no one would know. I'd put it back exactly as it was.

It's too much. I can't stop myself. I reach in and take his shirt off the hook. I hold it, run it through my hands. Imagine how it clung to Ray's body. I bring it up to my face and smell it. It's sweet, like perfume.

Then the realization washes over me. What am I doing? I feel like a stalker. Sniffing someone's shirt? Disgusting. *You creep*, I tell myself. *You sicko.*

Carefully, I hang Ray's shirt back up, and back away, walk right out of the locker room and back into the pool. I sit down on the metal bleachers and hang my head. I feel torn, torn between my desire for Ray and my own revulsion at that desire. Maybe it's because of the lack of sleep, but my head burns and I feel short of breath. There's a moment of deep silence inside me, and then the wave crashes, and I hold my head in my hands and cry. I keep crying until the first bell rings. I cry though first period. Then second period. My sobs echo against the tiles in the huge pool.

Finally, the well of tears dries up. I conjure up some reason to be late for school. My face is probably puffy and pale enough to look like I'm sick. I collect myself and leave through the back door, into the sunlight and fresh air.

Shrugging my backpack on, I walk around to the front entrance and sign in at the main office, which you have to do if you're coming in late. Nancy, the office administrator, looks at me suspiciously through her bifocals. She takes the clipboard after I'm done with it and reads what I've written. Then looks back at me. "You don't look sick," she says sharply, pulling a pencil from her immaculately permed mass of graying hair and initialing next to my name.

"Well, I guess I'm feeling better now," I say, making my voice a little hoarse.

"Get to class," she says. I go to the bathroom instead to wait out the rest of second period. I don't want to walk into bio lab halfway through. Amanda's my lab partner, and probably pissed that I'm not there to help sort out the male and female fruit flies. In the bathroom, I pull my phone from my backpack. Just as I suspected.

where r u?
hellooooo??
get your ass here already
charlie????

I splash some water on my face and look into the graffiti-covered mirror. I can barely make out my features between all the tags and childishly scrawled dicks. It doesn't matter, though. I don't even want to look at myself.

The bell rings, and kids start to pour out into the hall. I take a deep breath, stand up straight, and prepare to walk into English class and face whatever humiliation Mr. Mack has in store for me, not to mention undergoing the usual torment of sitting directly behind Ray.

It turns out that I only receive the usual public shaming every other student gets from Mack (as we call him) when they don't do their homework. I'd receive late credit if I could answer one question:

"When was Shakespeare born?" Mack asks me with his arms crossed, staring sternly into my eyes.

"April...twenty-third," I answer, a little unsure.

"Year?" Mack insisted.

I hesitate, thought. Then Ray turns around and smiles encouragingly at me. Like magic, the answer pops into my head.

"1564!" I say, a little too eagerly.

"Very good. Now, everyone turn to Act 1, Scene 2, please. Except for Charles, who is lacking his text today. Will someone share their book with poor Charles?" I hate when Mack calls me Charles.

"Sure," Ray says. Oh, God. He and I rearrange our chairs so they're next to each other, and he splays *Hamlet* open between us.

As Mack carries on with his lesson, I can barely follow along. I keep telling myself not to turn my head, keep my eyes on the text, pretend like Ray isn't there. Pretend I can't faintly hear his breathing, see his chest rise and fall out of the corner of my eye. Pretend like I can't smell that Ray smell, the same way the shirt in his locker smelled. Pretend like my heart doesn't skip a beat when Mack asks us to read a page of dialogue together as Hamlet and Horatio. "As you two already look like bosom friends," Mack says, and the class laughs.

Getting ready to leave at the end of class, I shyly mutter a "Thanks" to Ray.

"Sure thing, Charlie," he says, smiling that knee-weakening smile. "How are you feeling about the race?"

"Race?" I ask, confused.

"Our meet. Against Chester? It's next Sunday."

"Oh, yeah," I say, embarrassed, letting out a half-hearted laugh. I had genuinely forgot all about it. "I'm feeling good. I mean, I think I got the 1500 in the bag."

"Yeah? You sound pretty confident. How about a practice run tomorrow?"

Is he serious? "Uh, sure," I say. "On the field?"

"Nah, Frank'd probably pop out of nowhere and yell at us for being on school property on a Saturday. I'm pretty sure he lives under the bleachers or something. What about the tracks?"

"You mean the train tracks?" I ask.

"Yeah, why not? I measured on Google Maps, between the bridge and the old signal light is exactly 1500 meters. I mean, I was planning on running it myself. But I wouldn't mind the company."

"Sure, great," I reply. "Sounds like a date." *Oh shit*, I think, *did that really come out of my mouth? I meant "sounds like a plan!"*

But Ray just laughs. "Cool. So, noon at the bridge?"

"Yeah, I'll see you there," I say, and scurry out of the classroom.

Me. Ray. Together. Alone. Tomorrow.

Good God, I think. *What did I just agree to?*

At lunch, I barely touch my hastily made peanut butter and jelly sandwich. Amanda, as per usual, has her elaborate bento box of healthy non-GMO certified organic vegan food that she prepares herself every morning, complete with chopsticks. She pops something fluorescent beige into her mouth. I did not know it was possible for anything to be fluorescent beige.

"What the hell is that?" I ask, my nose curled in disgust.

"Tofu, dickhole," she says, her mouth full. Next to her, Josh takes an exaggeratedly huge bite of his cheeseburger, leaning close to Amanda and making hungry, carnivorous noises.

"Get the fuck out of here!" she says, pushing him away. Josh and I laugh. Amanda and I sit with a semi-rotating cast of cafeteria characters at lunchtime: Josh, obnoxious but kind-hearted; Violet and Iris, identical twins who usually study throughout lunch while picking at salads; and Jared and Samantha, who've been dating since birth and can never keep their hands off each other. Simon and Jake sometimes sit with us, too, especially when they've been kicked out of another table for flinging too much food at each other.

Ray has his own group of friends. Our social circles don't really intersect. He sits with most of the track team and some of the other kids who play sports. I'm a bit of an outlier among the Carlisle High athletics department and don't hang out with them too much. I get the sense they think I'm a little strange. But whatever, most of them are brain-dead jocks, anyways.

It turns out that Danny had taken my binder and book from my locker after I left, intending to text me to let me know he had them, but then promptly forgot all about it. He means well, but he's an airhead. He found me at lunch to return everything. "See ya, Charlie," he says as he walks away. "See ya, Blue," he says to Amanda. He always nicknames her based on the color of her hair. As he leaves, I look at Amanda and give her a goofy, wide-eyed grin.

"What?" she snaps. I keep staring at her with that stupid look she hates. "Oh, for fuck's sake," she grumbles, and takes another bite of her seaweed salad. But I can tell she's blushing.

"*See ya, Bluuuue,*" I mock, egging Amanda on. "When are the two of you gonna start acting more like *them?*" I ask, gesturing toward Jared and Samantha, enthusiastically making out. Vice Principal Gould walks by and yells at them to cut it out.

"You know I'm saving myself for marriage, Charlie," Amanda jokes.

"And apparently you're destined for Sean," I retort. "I still can't believe you're going to homecoming with him."

"Yeah, and *you're coming too,*" she says between clenched teeth. "Don't you even think of abandoning me to the fates."

"Okay, okay," I say.

"You know you need to find someone to go with, right? Don't you dare come sad and alone."

"Who, then?" I ask.

"I dunno. Ask Iris or Violet," Amanda says, pointing her chopsticks at them. I look over. They're chewing in sync and turn the pages of their textbooks at the exact same time. "Only a few more days to get tickets," Amanda reminds me. "Anyways, what the hell happened to you this morning?"

Just as I'm about to make up some story about being sick, Sean Costa walks over, visibly nervous. He keeps combing his hand through his thick red hair, causing it to stick out at all kinds of angles. "Uh, hey Amanda," he says.

Amanda sighs. "Hi, Sean," she says.

"Um, I'm supposed to ask you, I mean, I wanted to know, well, my mom said to ask, I mean—"

"What is it, Sean?" Amanda interrupts.

"So, what color is the dress that you're going to wear to homecoming? Cuz I'm supposed to, like, wear the same color?" He looks like he's bracing himself to get smacked.

"This isn't prom, Sean," Amanda answers. "And who says I'm wearing a dress? That's very heteronormative thinking, Sean. Maybe I'll come in a tuxedo."

"Oh, no, I mean, that's cool! Like, whatever you want. Thanks!" Sean practically runs away.

"Man, you have him wrapped around your little finger," I say to Amanda.

"I know," she grins. "I kinda like it."

The bell rings, and I toss my uneaten sandwich in the garbage.

"There are starving children in Cambodia, you know," Amanda yells to me over the noise of everyone migrating out of the cafeteria.

"Whatever," I answer, used to her social justice guilt trips. "I think we're making fudge brownies in Home Ec today. Gotta carb up for running." And I lose myself in the crowd before she can ask me again about this morning. Amanda always knows when I'm lying to her, and I can't even begin to think what I'd actually tell her. I trust Amanda, and so I'm afraid of saying something to her I might regret. It's not that she'd have any negative reaction if I came out to her. Actually, she'd probably give me a big hug and tell me everything's going to be all right. But that's the last thing I need right now. What I need is to disappear.

Chapter 4

Exhausted as I am, I can't get to sleep tonight. All that's on my mind is Ray. What was I thinking, agreeing to meet up with him tomorrow? What am I going to do? *Stay cool, Charlie*, I tell myself. *It's just a run.*

I try reading *Hamlet* in the hopes it'll put me to sleep, but that doesn't work. I keep reading the same lines over and over, my mind constantly drifting elsewhere. Even Mom could tell something was up. Over our pizza dinner, she kept asking me if I felt all right. I insisted I was fine. I scarfed down half a pizza, partly to keep my mouth occupied so I wouldn't have to talk and partly because I was starved from skipping lunch.

Then she dropped one of her classic Mom lines: "Honey, if anything's ever wrong, you know you can talk to me, don't you?"

"Yeah, I know," I mumbled.

"Anything, sweetie." She looked at me, concerned.

"Thanks, Mom," I said and got up to scrub my dishes in the sink before closing myself in my room to finish my overdue English homework.

So here I lie, restless, listening to the night wind rattle the dry autumn leaves outside my window. Replaying Ray's words in my head, over and over. *How about a practice run tomorrow?* And then my stupid answer. *Sounds like a date!* I can't stop mentally beating myself up for that one. Again and again the whole scene loops in my memory, until, eventually, my eyelids grow heavy and I fall asleep dreaming of Ray's smile.

It's just cold enough outside that I can see my breath as a faint steam when I exhale. I'm waiting at the tracks by the old bridge that spans a gulley in the woods. The sky is slate gray, and leaves fall like huge snowflakes every time the wind blows. I had put a sweatshirt on before leaving the house, but in my running shorts I'm still cold enough that I can feel my legs crawl with goosebumps. My chattering teeth, though—that's from nervousness, not the cold.

I pace anxiously on the tracks, stretch my legs, pace, stretch, pace. Check my watch. 12:01. I look around, unsure of which direction Ray will be coming from.

"Hey!" I hear behind me, and I jump back a bit, startled. I turn to see Ray walking up the embankment, along the path that's been beaten bare by so many feet taking this shortcut over so many years. "Sorry! Didn't mean to scare you." He's wearing a jacket with the hood pulled up. "It's cold," he says as he approaches where I stand.

"Yeah, pretty chilly," I say. Ray bends his knee and grabs his foot behind him, stretching out his thigh.

"Thanks for coming," he says. "I'm tired of running in circles during practice." He begins stretching the other leg.

"No problem. I like running here, especially in the fall." Ray bends over to touch his toes. I stare for one second longer than I mean to, and quickly look up into the treetops.

"You stretched, right? Good. Let's go!" And Ray starts running. I'm caught off guard, and it takes me a few seconds to register that I'm supposed to run, too.

I know Ray's a good runner, and we usually make about the same time at practice and at meets. But I also know that Ray is better at short-distance sprints, and weaker at longer distances. He can crush a 500-meter dash, but the 1500? That's more my territory. Even though he has a five-second head start, it's not long before I start to tail him pretty close. The trees whiz by in a blur of bright colors. After about a minute, I'm close enough that I can hear him breathing his careful, measured breaths. His legs pump the ground powerfully, but I have the longer stride. After another minute, I'm shoulder to shoulder with Ray. We both look at each other and smile. "Shit," Ray says between increasingly labored breaths. "How'd you get here so fast?"

"Less talking, more running," I say cockily. At that, Ray begins to speed up. Big mistake. I know you have to stay pretty consistently on pace for the 1500 or else you risk exhausting yourself too soon. We round a bend and have to duck to avoid getting hit in the face by an oak branch. We must be over halfway through, because I know that the rusted signal light isn't much farther. I can feel my lungs start to burn. I must be running faster than I ever have, fast enough to beat the devil. Then, just as I suspected, Ray starts to flag. I inch closer until we're beside each other again. Both of us are panting heavily, the cold air driving into our chests like ice crystals. I can see the signal light ahead now, and in one final explosive push, I overtake Ray and pass the signal a second before he does.

We both slow to a halt, out of breath, coughing, bent over with our hands on our knees trying to regain control of our lungs. I can feel my torso covered in a cold sweat beneath my sweatshirt. Our coughing and panting eventually turns to laughing. "Jesus," Ray says once he can finally talk. "That had to've been your fastest run ever. Did you time it?"

I had forgot to start my stopwatch, of course. "Forgot," I manage to get out, and we both laugh again. Gradually, our breathing returns to normal.

"I gotta sit down," Ray says and walks over to an enormous tree stump. I decide to join him. We sit close together on the stump, only a foot, maybe, of room between us. We're both quiet. I look at Ray, furtively. Sweat has matted down his curly hair somewhat, and a drop of it runs down his temple. A swarm of butterflies decides to wake up in my stomach, and I turn away.

"You know," Ray says, "when I run, it's like the only time I'm really, like, *here*, y'know? Like I can forget about everything. Except running. Just me and the ground and the air."

"I know what you mean," I answer. "You don't have to worry about anything except getting to the finish line." I shift my position on the stump to get more comfortable. When I set my hand down, it accidentally lands on top of Ray's. Instinct tells me immediately to pull it away, but for the first time, maybe ever, another part of me speaks up. The part of me that says to leave my hand right where it is.

Ray doesn't move. He doesn't look at me, either. Maybe he doesn't realize, or maybe he thinks I don't realize and he's too embarrassed to point it out. My heart races almost as quickly as it did during the run. Ten seconds go by, then twenty, before that other part of me, the part that hates itself, insists that I pull my hand away. So I do, slowly, and set it back down on the stump.

Then Ray says something completely unexpected: "It's okay, Charlie." And he turns to me. And I turn to him. We look at each other in complete silence. Something in me calms. His dark eyes are warm. A half-smile plays on his lips, like always. "Charlie," he says, "it's *okay*." I look away, then inch my hand back over to his, and set it back on top. We remain that way for a while, silent, my hand on his. His thumb moves, slowly, and caresses the side of my hand.

Things slow down. Something prompts us both to look at each other. A raw energy pulses between us. And then, somehow, our lips are pressed together. Somehow, we're kissing. And it's the single most beautiful feeling in the world. It's like running, but better. My eyes closed, the rest of the world slips away, until there's just me, and Ray, and the soft fullness of his lips on mine.

We both pull away at the same time, open our eyes. I can feel a part of me tear away as we separate: inhibition, fear, regret. I lean forward and kiss him again. He presses his mouth back, a harder kiss this time, and reaches his other hand up and brings it to hold the side of my face. I bring my own hand up to the back of his head, tangle my fingers through the soft curls of his hair. This kiss lasts a long while.

Eventually, we separate. We both exhale little clouds.

"Thank you," I whisper. It seems like the right thing to say.

"Sure," Ray whispers back. Then, springing onto his feet, he says, "So we're racing back to the bridge, right?" And before I can answer, he's already sprinting off. This time, it doesn't take me as long to start running after him.

Chapter 5

Ray and I parted ways back at the bridge (I beat him, again), rather awkwardly. "This was fun, Charlie," he said. "I'll see you later." And he walked off down the embankment.

I've been puzzling over these last words all day. I mean, after what happened, it seemed kind of a weird thing to say. What *did* happen, anyways? Well, besides the obvious. Does Ray have feelings for me, too? Or was this just a one-time thing? Is Ray gay? Is he *out*? Nobody's ever seemed to mention it. And that's the kind of thing people in school would *definitely* mention.

Walking home, I feel lighter than air. I can still feel Ray on my lips, a tingle that won't go away. And I can't stop smiling. When I get home, I flop down on my bed, and all at once, the exhaustion of the past few days catches up with me, and I don't wake up until Mom comes home. For a split second, I think the whole thing had been a dream—the woods, the run, the kiss—but then reality comes flooding back, and I bounce out of my room.

"Well, you're looking better today," Mom says when she sees me.

"Yeah, I feel great! I mean, I'm fine," I answer, a little too enthusiastically. We have dinner in front of the TV and spend our Saturday night watching Netflix and eating microwave popcorn.

When I wake up the next day, I feel like I need to go back to the train tracks. Take a walk to clear my head. I bring *Hamlet* with me, figure I'll find somewhere to sit and work on that monologue. Maybe that same stump from yesterday.

The sun is out, and the sky is a summertime shade of blue. I make my way leisurely down the road toward the wooded embankment where the tracks are. It's even more beautiful here than yesterday. The reds and oranges of the leaves paint the sky with a palette of fire. Everything seems so fresh to me, so open.

As I walk down the tracks through the tunnel of trees, I think about how I feel. It's far from how I would have expected to feel. It's different from that feeling of revulsion and self-loathing after handling Ray's shirt. Different from my feelings of embarrassment in the locker room. Different from how I feel I always need to hide from Mom and from Amanda. That open act of intimacy felt wonderful. Perfectly natural. It didn't feel wrong, or unwanted. It opened my eyes to the possibility of feeling at home in my own body. To the possibility of living without shame.

I arrive at the old battered signal light, and beyond it, the stump. I stop dead in my tracks—there, sitting on the stump, is Ray. He sees me, too, and waves. A surge of joy rushes through me. "What are you doing here?" I ask as I walk up to him.

"I don't know, I just felt like I needed to be here. And I felt like I knew you'd be here, too."

"Y'know, I kinda felt the same way." I sit down next to him. "Well, actually, I was planning on practicing my monologue for Mack's class."

"Need help?" he asks.

"Sure," I say, opening the book to my scene and handing it over to him. "It's the one that's underlined. And highlighted. And starred."

Ray laughs. "Go ahead," he says.

"*Oh, that this too too solid flesh would melt,*" I begin, "*Thaw, and resolve itself into a*...uh…"

"Dew," Ray prompts.

"Thanks. *Into a dew. Or that the Everlasting had not fix'd his canon gainst self-murder—*"

"Self-*slaughter,*" Ray interrupts, but I hear a hitch in his voice and look over to see tears running down his cheeks.

"Ray?" I ask. "Ray? What's wrong? Hey, it's okay." I put my hand on his back to comfort him, but he shrugs it off. He almost *flinches.*

"Charlie, I'm so sorry," he says through tears. "Yesterday...what we did...it was all wrong. I shouldn't have done that to you."

"You didn't *do anything* to me, Ray," I say. "I wanted that to happen. And I think I have for a long time."

37

"You don't understand," Ray almost shouts and stands up quickly. "I...I'm not...I mean, I never told anyone I'm…" He can barely find the words through his tears, through his anger. "You can't tell anyone. If anyone knew...if my parents knew...I don't know what I'd do. I couldn't live with myself. Charlie, we can't do this. We can't talk about this. Ever. It didn't happen. Okay?"

"Ray, I...I don't understand. You seemed...so happy yesterday."

"That's the problem, Charlie. I was. Happy. But I shouldn't be. Because what we did, it's just...wrong."

"It didn't *feel* wrong, Ray. It felt...*perfect.*"

"I have to go. Please, Charlie. Just forget it happened." And he turns, walks around the bend in the tracks, and is gone.

I sat there, unable to move or speak or even breathe. I thought Ray and I felt the same way about what happened. There was such a spark between us yesterday, such joy. Where I felt liberated, Ray felt crushed. The complete opposite of what I expected.

Well, what did you expect? I think. It's back, now, that awful, nagging part of me. *Did you think you two would fall in love? Become boyfriends? Get married? Of course not. This was never going to work. You just should've stayed away from him.* But Ray made the first move, didn't he? He said it was okay. He seemed so sure, so confident. But now...now I don't know what he is. Or what *we* are.

Most of all, I feel sorry for Ray. Sad that he didn't find as much joy in our kiss as I did. That he doesn't see it for the beautiful thing it is.

I can feel the doubt creeping back in. I wonder if I hadn't just spun up an illusion that it was all so wonderful, told myself a story about the connection between us. Maybe there never was a connection. Maybe my feelings for Ray, and my feelings for any boy, can only ever lead to disappointment.

Ray left my copy of *Hamlet* on the stump. Before I leave, I pick it up, noticing that it's still open to my monologue. I look closer, and find that a few of Ray's tears have stained the page, right beside the last line: *But break, my heart; for I must hold my tongue.*

Chapter 6

The next week passes painfully slow. I wake up every morning feeling like I weigh a thousand pounds, dragging myself out of bed. I ask Amanda if she can pick me up and give me a ride. I can't bring myself to walk to school, walk along those tracks where Ray and I ran, past that stump where we kissed, and, later, where Ray let his mask slip to reveal his true, vulnerable, broken self.

"Morning, sunshine," Amanda says as I get into her car Monday morning. "Mr. Emo doesn't want to go on his lonesome, contemplative walk through the woods today?"

"No, he doesn't," I answer. "Thanks for picking me up."

We drive along in silence. It's a foggy morning, and wet droplets cling to the windshield and drip down like tears.

"You all right?" Amanda asks. I knew this was coming.

"Fine. Just tired." Silence again.

"You're a terrible liar, Charlie," she says.

"Just leave it, okay?" I snap.

"Nah. I don't think I will." And Amanda pulls over to the side of the road and puts her ancient Beetle in park. "We're not moving until you tell me what's going on. You were acting weird last week, and you're acting weird today. Charlie, if something's wrong, you can tell me. Honestly."

"Amanda, will you please just drive? I really don't want to be late."

"I think the fruit flies and Punnett squares can wait a few minutes." Silence. "So?"

"Amanda, I…" I turn and look at her. I can feel the words coming up my throat. It would be so easy. But I swallow them back down. "I just had a rough few days. I thought…I thought I knew someone. But it turns out I don't. Not really."

"Jesus, Charlie, you didn't ask someone to homecoming and get rejected, did you? Because if that's the case, you're blowing it way out of proportion."

"It's not that, Amanda. It's hard to explain." I really want her to start driving again. Get to school, get out of the car, lose myself in the crowd.

"All right, suit yourself," Amanda says, yanking the car back in gear and flooring it. We zoom along a good twenty miles above the speed limit, and the car swerves and shrieks into the school parking lot, almost running over a few kids along the way. Amanda slams the breaks and the car skids to a halt in her parking spot. "Out," she says and nearly shoves me through the door.

Like I said, the next few days pass slowly. I pass Ray in the halls a few times, and we don't make eye contact, pretend we're invisible. Mack's class is the worst, because I have to sit behind him. Forty interminable minutes of looking at the back of his head, his hair through which I had run my fingers while we kissed. At the end of class, he gets up and runs out of the room like he's about to miss a train. Practice is even worse. I make horrible time all week, and Coach Fielder does nothing but yell at me.

Ray, though, has been running like hell. Like he's channeling all his fear and frustration into trying to get to the finish line faster than the speed of sound. Then, there's the relay. I'm up second, and Ray's up third, which means I have to pass the baton to him. He waits in his starting stance as I approach, not as quickly as I could be doing, when he yells, "C'mon, Charlie, hurry up!" Anger fills his voice, and he rips the baton out of my hand and flies away.

Then, Friday. Our last practice before the meet at Chester on Sunday. I make shit time, and Ray makes the best out of anyone. So of course, the locker room is filled alternately with praise for Ray and nothing but jeers at my expense.

"The hell is wrong with you, Charlie? Your 1500 was crap."

"You're gonna crush it at Chester, Ray."

"Charlie, if you don't pick up the pace, Coach'll keep you on the sidelines."

"You might take us to state, Ray!"

And on and on. Each time someone says something, I can feel a little ball of white fire grow hotter behind my forehead. Eventually, the discussion turns elsewhere.

"Hey, you have that speech memorized?" Simon asks Jake.

"Shit! No. When're we supposed to have it ready?" Jake asks.

"Monday, dipshit."

"Can't I just pay one of the theatre kids to do it for me? I'll just ask Mack if Lisa or someone can be my, uh, what's it called...surrajet? I'm pretty sure she has the hots for me."

"Surrogate, dumbass. And Lisa's a dyke."

"Oh, right, she does theatre! Why's drama club always filled with fags?"

"Who knows. I guess being dramatic just comes naturally to them. Hey, Charlie, do you have yours memorized?"

"Yeah," I mumble, shoving my uniform in my bag.

"Well, look at you," Jake says sarcastically. "Why don't you join the theatre fags?"

"Maybe you are one," Simon sneers. "You run like a fag."

"Ha! Yeah! Maybe that's what he is, huh, Charlie?" Jake pokes my shoulder, hard. "You a fag now?"

Sitting on the bench, I feel something in me pop. Shatter. Spots dance in front of my eyes. "Yes," I say under my breath.

"What?" Simon asks.

Louder now, I say, "Yes."

"Yes, what? What's your deal?"

I stand up, turn to face Simon and Jake, who stand staring at me in their underwear. "Yes," I say. "I am."

"What?" Jake asks.

"I'm a fag, Jake. That what you want to hear?" I start getting louder, and the locker room quiets down. "How's that? I'm gay. I like boys. Hey, maybe I'm into the two of you." Simon and Jake look like deer caught in headlights. They've gone slack-jawed, and the color drains from their faces. Mine only grows hotter. "I'm sick of both of your shit. Yeah, I'm gay. And I don't appreciate the two of you using that word all the damn time." The locker room was so quiet you could hear a pin drop. "So there. Happy? I'm gay. And you two can go fuck yourselves." I swing my backpack on and get ready to walk out. "Actually, maybe you two should get it over with already and fuck each other." I didn't know it was possible for a room to get as silent as the vacuum of space.

I turn and head for the door. Before I leave, I see Ray, standing still, watching me. I pause and look at him directly in the eyes. He has a look of astonishment on his face, but behind that, I almost sense a look of pride. But I know my face is still a mask of anger. I hope he sees that. And I turn and leave, slamming the door behind me.

Even though school is out for the weekend, I know word of what I did will spread like wildfire via text and phone calls and Facebook. I just committed what's known as "social suicide." And I couldn't care less.

As I knew would happen, Amanda calls me an hour after I get home. I don't answer. She keeps calling until I turn my phone off and get into the shower. I make the water as hot as it can get without actually burning and scrub myself with soap, trying to wash everything away. I stand under the showerhead until the hot water runs out, then towel off and get dressed back in my room.

"Charlie?" Mom's voice. I didn't hear her come home.

"Yeah?" I call back.

"Charlie, Amanda called the house looking for you." Of course she did. "She sounded pretty worried. Is everything all right?"

"It's fine, Mom, thanks," I call back. "It's just...homework stuff. She's having trouble with calculus. Guess I didn't hear my phone go off." I couldn't sound more unconvincing. I hear the telltale creaks of the hallway floor, letting me know Mom's coming to my room.

Quietly, now, right on the other side of the closed door, she says, "Charlie. Please open the door. Whatever's going on...we need to talk."

I stand still. Take a deep breath. Open the door. The look of concern, of pain, and of love in Mom's eyes is overwhelming. This is hurting her even more than it's hurting me.

"You're right, Mom," I say. "We do."

It's midnight as I walk to the playground. I don't know how I managed to sneak out of the house, creeping like Spider-Man, avoiding all the creaks and groans and slipping out the back door. The night is clear, and cold. The crescent moon is bright, high in the sky. I can make out Orion and the Big Dipper. My dad taught me to recognize them, a long time ago.

Eighteen missed calls and twenty-seven texts. All from Amanda. I scrolled through them all, not bothering to read them except for the last one:

be at the playground @ midnight. please, charlie. it's important.

I know it's not fair to Amanda to treat her like this. And what's the use of trying to sleep, anyways? I can't let Amanda just wait at the playground by herself, at midnight. And she knows I can't possibly be that cruel. So, here I am.

I spot Amanda's bright blue hair and see she's sitting on one of the swings. But she's not alone. Someone's sitting on the swing next to her.

It's Ray.

I shiver, wrap my coat a bit more tightly around me, and slowly walk up to them.

"Hey, stranger," Amanda says softly, kindly.

"Hey," I say.

"I called her, Charlie," Ray says. "Well, I asked Iris to ask Danny to ask Sean for her number."

"God only knows how Sean even got my number, the creep, because *I* didn't give it to him."

"I told her everything. I told her I needed to see you."

46

"Nice guy, this one," Amanda says. "A keeper." And she winks.

"Y'know, she's pretty cool, Charlie," Ray says.

"Why thank you, Ray. Sometimes I think Charlie just doesn't appreciate my valuable presence in his life."

"Can we talk, Charlie?" Ray asks, a pleading look in his eyes.

"Well, I'll be at the carousel if anyone needs me," Amanda says, getting up and walking away. I take a seat on the swing she vacated, next to Ray.

"Charlie," Ray starts, "I'm so sorry. About how I acted. About how I treated you."

"There's nothing to apologize for, Ray," I say, and I mean it. "I know what it's like. To hate yourself that much."

A moment of silence passes between us, broken only by the song of crickets. We both sway gently in our swings.

"What happened in the locker room...I know what you said was out of anger. And those two deserved it. But, I mean...is it true? Do you think...I mean...are you?"

"Gay?" I say. "Yeah. I mean, I'm pretty sure. I've been pretty sure for a long time. And I really didn't expect that that's how I'd come out."

"Yeah, me neither," Ray says, and laughs. "I guess...well, I saw what you did, and it made me, I don't know. Sad. But also glad. And proud. That you could say that. Say something I'd never be able to."

"Ray, I don't know you all that well," I say. "I don't know what you're family is like, what your friends are like, what you've been through. But believe me. You can. You don't have to make a scene like I did. Obviously. But when you're ready, it's a terrific feeling." Silence again. "So," I ask, "what's the talk around town been like?"

"Unending," Ray laughs. "Look at this," and he pulls out his phone, scrolls through his group texts from a dozen people. A lot of them are guys on the team. A lot of them aren't. All I see is "Charlie" and "gay" written over and over and look away. "I don't know what I'm going to do when I get back to school. And I should probably skip the meet Sunday."

"No, Charlie," Ray says, handing his phone over to me. "*Look.*" And I do. And I realize that, yes, while some of the texts are less than kind, a lot of them mention how I "*put those assholes in their place,*" how people want to "*reach out to charlie and make sure hes ok.*" It's not as bad as I thought it would be. Not at all.

"Wow," I say, and hand the phone back. Silence, again. "I talked to my mom."

"Seriously?" Ray asks.

"Yeah. Told her everything."

"What happened?"

"Nothing. She told me how much she loved me. How she's so sorry how my dad used to treat me. It was...hard. But fine, in the end. We ordered Thai and watched *X-Files.*" Ray laughs.

"I can't do that," Ray says. "Not yet. I'm not ready to be, y'know, *out.* Not all the way. But maybe...maybe, to a few people. A few friends that I trust."

"I think that's a good start, Ray," I tell him and reach my hand out to rub the back of his neck. He turns his head around to face me, and my hand lands on his cheek. We both lean towards each other and kiss, gently. A little unsteadily, actually, since we are on swings.

"So what do we do?" he asks me, his face close to mine, his breath warm, fogging the space between us.

"I think we just take it one day at a time," I answer. And he leans forward and kisses me again. Our mouths parted slightly, we take in each other's breath.

From the other side of the playground, Amanda lets out a cheer. Ray and I both laugh, take each other's hands and truss our fingers together.

"One day at a time," Ray repeats. "I can do that."

We beat Chester on Sunday and are headed to the state championships next month. I made record time on the 1500, and Ray clinched the relay for us. Simon and Jake were sidelined because Coach Fielding eventually caught wind of what they said to me in the locker room. But on the bus ride back home, they both stood up and made a public apology to me, and to everyone. They promised never to say anything "homophobic or whatever" to me, or to anyone, ever again. And they ended their joint speech—clearly rehearsed, probably more than their Shakespeare monologues—by proclaiming together, "It's OK to be gay!" It was so sincere, but so theatrical, that everyone laughed at them and gave them a round of applause, and they both took a bow and promptly toppled over into the aisle when the bus came to a sudden stop.

I spend more time with Mom, now, and less time locked in my room. We talk a lot, about the past, the future. Things we never said to each other but always wanted to.

I did go to homecoming, without a date. Ray went too, with Violet. Danny snuck in some vodka, and Amanda and Sean and Ray and I all drank some in the bathroom until the little flask was empty. Amanda and Sean made a pretty cute couple, actually. But Violet just ended up spending the entire dance gossiping with Iris, and Amanda ended up making out with Danny in a broom closet, and Sean spent the evening doing the Macarena to every song with his theatre friends.

And Ray and I...well, we're not boyfriends. I'm not sure what we are, right now. And that's okay. We have time to figure things out.

But then, at the end of the night, the most amazing thing happens. The last few songs are playing, and couples start slow dancing. I'm sitting down, picking at a brownie Amanda had abandoned upon disappearing with Danny. Ray comes over to me and holds out his hand.

"What?" I ask, confused. "You want some brownie?"

Ray just laughs. "No," he says. "I want to dance." I'm speechless. "C'mon, Charlie, before the music stops and I change my mind."

I stand up and take Ray's hand. He leads me to the dance floor, puts one hand around my hip and tells me to do the same to him. "Sorry, I've never slow danced before," I say.

"It's all right," Ray says. "Just follow my lead."

So we danced, Ray and I. And nobody seemed to mind. The other couples smiled at us. Two boys in suits, slow dancing to some cheesy song from the nineties.

"One day at a time," Ray whispers into my ear. I look into his incredible, perfect, beautiful eyes.

Smiling, I whisper back, "I can do that."

Written in the Journal (Clay's Story)

This isn't a place I ever expected to be in.

When I close my eyes, all I can see are my family's faces staring at me. Or at least, what I think their faces will look like when I tell them. And when I'm in bed trying to get some of this "sleep" I hear everyone talking about, all I can hear are those things I heard my friends say to the kids at school. Not usually to their faces, more so when we're all together somewhere else.

But even my friends don't know, because I haven't told them, because I'm scared.

This is what I wrote before I knew what to do with myself. I was at school when I wrote it, just before Miss Ingram's math class. That day I was feeling particularly alone, even though there were a lot of people around me. I had so much more to write—some people think it's weird that I enjoy writing so much, since I guess most 18-year-old guys don't do it.

I was about to write more, but I heard the voices of my friends and I quickly tore the page out, crumpling it up and shoving it into my back pocket. Just in time, too. They were right behind me, laughing and slapping me on the back, telling me I had to come watch the girls' soccer practice after school ended because Madison would be there along with her posse. Everyone knew they were the hottest girls at school. I didn't see much in them.

…because I'm scared.

That's the whole reason I bore this burden alone for so long. I was scared. Fearful out of my mind, really. It didn't make sense to me. What's so shameful about being gay? I didn't ask for it. There should be no reason for me, or anyone else, to conceal such a thing from everyone, like it was some massive secret that would get me arrested or something.

Carrying the weight of something so trivial, something that shouldn't even be an issue in the world because it's not harming anyone, poisoned me. Drove me mad.

But even as I thought and felt all these things, I still couldn't shake the feeling that, because I'm gay, I'm a failure since my love life involves other guys and not girls like everyone expects where I'm from. The feeling that I'm a shame in and of myself. Which of course isn't true. I'm confident enough to say that now.

What's sad is how a lot of people who aren't straight feel this way, like their identity is flawed. I can make all these claims because I've felt all these things so strongly before.

There were a lot of reasons these thoughts were so firmly rooted in my head. The first incident that comes to mind is one about a year ago.

I was walking with a couple of my friends, Eron and Bailey, after school. We had just taken our midterm tests that day, and we were all so tired because we had procrastinated studying until the end of last week. Obviously, we brought the trouble on ourselves and had to pull three or four all-nighters to get all our lost studying time in. After being cooped up in a classroom all day, it felt good to get outside and walk around in the fresh air. (Secretly we hoped it would refresh us and magically make us get 100s on all our tests the next day.)

"I don't think I did so good on that last one," complained Eron.

"History?" I asked.

"Doesn't sound like you did so hot on your grammar, either," laughed Bailey. Eron gave him a questioning look, to which Bailey explained, "It's 'you did well,' not 'you did good.'"

"Grammar nerd," I pushed him off the sidewalk playfully.

"Says the writer!"

"Okay, okay, break it up!" Eron came between us and put his arms over our shoulders. "The real question, boys, is what do you think of Sara?"

Bailey made a throw-up noise. "Not Sara, man! She was like our bro, except a girl."

"We haven't hung out with her in forever, though," I pointed out.

"That's why I said *was*."

I noticed Bailey give a look to Eron that was kind of sad. I had never been as close with Sara as they were, so I asked what happened.

"Ah, nothing." Eron kicked the ground, scattering rocks everywhere. "She just started hanging out with weird people. Just…kind of drifted away from us, I guess."

I tried to think of who they meant by "weird people" but came to no conclusion. My face must have been confused, because, without any hesitation, they gave me an answer.

"Those kids who do weird expressive arts, and the gays and lesbians."

Eron looked at Bailey and rolled his eyes. They snickered at the very idea of these people. I wish I hadn't seen or heard it. My eyes went blurry and immediately my mood crashed to the ground.

Bailey and Eron started talking about some poster they had seen around school advertising a club for experimental performance art, of course started by the "weird kids." But I couldn't hear what they were saying even though they were right in front of me. It felt like I was freezing and sweating at the same time.

"What kind of stuff do you think they'll do, Clay?" Eron asked me through a laugh.

"Oh…I don't know. Maybe some dance thing." I didn't know what else to say. They noticed I was acting different suddenly, and I told them it just sucks to have lost a good friend.

Luckily, at that time my phone rang to give me a distraction. It was my mom letting me know she was working the night shift at the hospital and she had left dinner in the oven.

Honestly, my first thought was how I'd be glad to have the house a little quieter tonight. Dad would be home, but he didn't ask much about school or feelings. Those are definitely more "mom questions."

Still a little down, I decided to use Mom's phone call to my advantage. I told Eron and Bailey I had to go home. We all turned around and walked back to our cars, yelling "See you tomorrow!" as we drove separate ways.

The rest of the night I barely said anything to anyone. I didn't even reply to any text messages my friends sent me. I tried to study but kept getting preoccupied with wondering why I'd been so affected by what they had said about Sara and the "weird kids." I even got out my notebook and tried to process my thoughts through writing, but it seemed the words were stuck and refused to come out.

Unable to do any studying the deeper in my mind I explored, I turned off all my lights and stared out the window for what seemed like hours. A streetlight was just outside; hundreds of bugs flew wildly around the light and bats began to swoop down quickly, enjoying the all-you-can-eat buffet. Something about the sight was calming.

I thought about my family and how they would react if I were to tell them that I was gay. I wondered how long I could live my life without telling them. I was about to leave the house anyway for college in a few months, and I would get a job in the summer to keep me busy. Deep down I was conflicted as to whether or not I could get away with hiding it, but I knew it would drive me crazy.

Turning back to my notebook, I opened it to start writing something, but my eyes caught on an entry I had written a few months ago. Almost like magic, it happened to be about my family and why I felt like I couldn't be honest with them about my sexuality. I skimmed over the entry several times, digesting what it said.

I think one of the reasons I'm terrified of coming out to my family is because they have come face-to-face with gay people, or anyone of any non-straight sexuality, very few times. It's not something they've been around much at all, so it's something they've never had to develop a rational opinion about. Covington isn't such a big city anyway, so I'm not surprised that it's still pretty taboo here. Or at least, it feels like it.

Growing up I never heard my parents talk about being gay. They never had any gay friends, and when something of the topic came up on TV, they would sigh and sometimes even roll their eyes. Like that had nothing to do with them, or they thought it was ridiculous. My grandparents said a couple of times that being gay isn't how nature intended it, and they were appalled that "homosexuals" were out and proud on the media.

My dad said one time, a long time ago, that people claim to be gay just to get attention. His words upset me, even though I was young. Maybe I knew then that I was gay. Maybe I didn't yet, but I knew that what he said wasn't true. He never said it again after that, but I remember it to this day unfortunately.

I don't want to have scars from their words.

I hope that one day, if I can ever manage to come out to them, they will accept me and love me…and my boyfriend whenever I have one. I hope that they will realize one reason they had these opinions is because they misunderstood people who aren't like them. And more than that, these people who are different are a group who my parents have never come into contact with.

Reading this entry was a strange experience for me. I vaguely remembered writing it, but how I read it now felt like someone else wrote it. It seemed like back a few months ago when I wrote it, I had been a lot more levelheaded about the whole thing. Really, I was even able to understand to some extent why my parents and grandparents had the ideas they did. This got me thinking: they grew up in a very different era, one that I can't relate to because I grew up with lots of gay people in the media.

Maybe it would be easy to come out now, I thought. And for a moment, my heart soared. After all, in this day and age, it's everywhere. It doesn't seem like it would be such a taboo thing. And if I were to come out, I definitely wouldn't be alone. There are thousands of people like me in films, on social media, at school…

She just started hanging out with weird people.

Ouch. It was like I heard Eron's voice so clearly in my head. Where my mood had just lifted a few seconds ago, there it dropped again. I was back in the same boat as before, and I felt anxious. My friends kind of sounded like my parents. Maybe their parents talked like that, and to be honest, the LGBT scene in my town was pretty nonexistent. I admired—and envied—the kids at school who were already out.

What am I supposed to do?

My heart hurt from what people I loved had said. I wondered if Eron and Bailey called the gay kids "weird" because they had never taken the time to get to know them. I wondered how it would be different if I came out. If I confessed to them that I was gay, would they feel guilty and embarrassed about the things they had said in front of me?

As I sat in front of the window with my head turned toward the streetlamp, I jolted and rubbed my eyes hard. I had gotten so lost in my mind that I hadn't blinked in a while, and my eyes burned. The whole time I'd had my eyes open in the direction of the bats' feast, but I hadn't seen any of it. How long had I been gone from my body?

A lot of feelings hit me like a ton of bricks, and I felt myself start shaking. Several times before I had experienced panic attacks, and I didn't want this to be one of them. I turned my lights back on, loaded up a good playlist, and got in the shower to rinse away everything I was worried about.

I stayed in the shower for a really long time. It felt good to close my eyes and let the water rush over me. I pretended that I was in a jungle under a waterfall. The jungle seemed like a safe place to be who I am and not worry about anything.

Screw studying, I thought. Tomorrow's exam was math, one of my best subjects, and we had already done a few mock tests. I was definitely ready for it, and I was proud of myself for wanting to do well on it. Last year I wouldn't have cared, but this year it hit me how important my grades were for getting into a good college.

But still, screw studying. I couldn't handle any more of it. I went into the kitchen and made myself a ham and cheese sandwich since I'd eaten dinner a long time ago. Dad was asleep in front of the TV, which played some boring news program. He woke up just as I was about to go to bed, and we told each other goodnight.

I didn't bother turning my lights on. This was becoming a pattern; I seemed to think more clearly and focus better without the lights, which sucked because it's impossible to study in the dark. I lay down on my bed and stared at the ceiling, hoping the dark thoughts wouldn't come back.

But they did. Pretty soon my mind started to wander in a million directions, and I felt my heart pick up the pace.

Pull it together, Clay, I commanded myself, but it was no use.

There was only one thing left to do: try to write it down. I got a brilliant idea as I tried to find a working pen on my desk. What if I wrote down everything I was scared of?

For a second, I was excited instead of nervous. Maybe this would be a way to let go of some of these negative feelings.

WHAT AM I AFRAID OF?

1. *My friends judging me.*
2. *My family judging me.*
3. *Who to come out to first?*
4. *If friends first, maybe they don't receive it well. Maybe they blab to the whole school that I'm gay and everyone thinks of me differently. And if they know first, my family might find out from someone else, and be angry I didn't tell them first.*
5. *If family first, maybe they'll worry that I've been hiding a relationship from them. Maybe they'll come up with their own stories in their heads and make other family members think differently.*
6. *Do I really need to come out during my senior year? Isn't that a really tough time to make huge life changes? Would it be easier to start college as a new person?*
7. *Maybe I'm not really gay.*

I wrote so fast my hand hurt, but I felt a weight almost literally lift off me. It felt so liberating to tell all my fears to someone, even if that someone was just a notebook.

With a deep breath, I looked at my short list. *I'm sure there will be more to add to it,* I thought. *But for now, it's good enough to settle me down.*

I set the alarm on my phone, took a long drink of water, and pulled the covers up to my neck. The 7th fear on my list was that I wasn't really gay, and yeah, it did cross my mind, but I had already worked through that idea a couple of years ago.

I am gay, I told myself sternly, *and I am just the same person as I've always been. It's not a crime. I'm not evil. It's okay to be how I am.*

Coming out, whenever I was going to do it, wouldn't be easy, that much was for sure. It would be nerve-wracking and courageous, but I had to be honest. If I was going to start college as a new person, I wanted to start off on the right foot.

They might tease me about Anne. I had dated Anne in sophomore year just because everyone wanted me to. She liked me, and I thought she was cool, but I wasn't into her in the dating way. At that time, I was still grappling with the truth of my sexuality, and I thought maybe if I tried dating her, I would figure out more about myself.

It's okay if they tease me about Anne. I popped my knuckles and thought about how Anne and I had fun together, but dating each other wasn't the best idea. We broke up after a couple of weeks. *The guys still tease me about her sometimes anyway. I don't think she would get teased if I came out.* She really is a cool girl, and we're still friends. Just…not my thing, romantically.

My mind started to collect more and more ideas and thoughts and, although I didn't feel so anxious this time, I had to do everything I could to shut it off so I could sleep.

Pause here, I made a mental note, *and resume all of this tomorrow.*

After all, I had a math exam to ace.

Chapter 2

Just that morning, I got a text from Anne.

She sent it at 5:30 a.m. I saw the message when I rolled over to turn my alarm off, and I didn't even understand what she had texted. In my sleepy head all I saw was the time she sent it.

Apparently I texted her, but I didn't know it until I was getting in the car to drive to school. *Why were you awake at 5:30?*

I'm running track now and we don't have practice today!

So whyw ere yuo awke at 5:30? (I was embarrassed to see this one.)

Text me later when you're awake, silly. Maybe see you at school.

OK

Reading back through the messages I was half-amused and half-humiliated at my fixation on why she was awake before sunrise. I didn't remember sending any of those messages. *I'll have to find her at school and explain,* I thought.

While I drove to school, I kept thinking about Anne. I didn't know why she kept popping into my head. She was the last person I was thinking about before falling asleep, but usually my thoughts don't carry over to the next morning.

In a few minutes, it hit me. I was worried about her, and the reason I was worried about her was because…

My heart stopped, and I got a chill down my back. I kind of felt lightheaded, like I was going to throw up. *I think I'm actually considering coming out.*

It only makes sense, right? If I wasn't thinking about coming out, I wouldn't be worried about Anne. The only reason we dated is because everyone thought we should. We were pretty good friends. She's really gorgeous and has great fashion sense, and we always hung out together in our big group of friends.

Not only that, but we also have lots of stories together. The first time I ever had a beer was with her at a party we stumbled across on the beach, and luckily for us we look older than we actually are. The beer was disgusting, and she and I ran away as soon as we could get those drunk strangers to quit talking to us.

It started with her friends and mine conspiring behind our backs that we liked each other, even though I'm convinced I never gave out any romantic vibes (back during this time, I was really confused about having attractions to guys and not girls). Maybe she did, but I never picked up on it. Obviously.

Her friends talked to her and my friends teased me for a few weeks until the pressure built up so much that Anne and I had to get together privately to talk about it. We didn't want to break our friendship, but we decided, why not try it out? Maybe we were too caught up in our heads to notice that we liked each other.

At the same time Anne and I were having this conversation, a million thoughts were running through my head. This can be expected because I knew—in retrospect, I know this for certain—that I was gay. I knew I loved Anne as a close friend I'd known for years, as someone I had a lot of fun with, but I knew I didn't love her in the way our friends wanted me to love her. I can't speak for her, of course, but that's how I felt.

Some other thoughts were more flashbacks of my friends making jokes about gay people or scoffing in the direction of the few gay kids who had come out at school. You know how people say, "That's so gay!" when something ridiculous is mentioned. I hate that phrase, and I never knew why I hated it until I realized…I'm gay.

When Anne and I were figuring out what to do and my head was getting caught up in all these thoughts and memories, I felt a fear open up inside me that all I'd end up doing is breaking Anne's heart eventually. Apparently I spaced out and my eyes glassed over the more I thought about these things, and she had to wave her hand in front of my face.

"Clay?" she asked. "You okay?"

I snapped out of it. "Yeah, I was just thinking about it all. And I'm tired."

Why did I say that? I yelled at myself. This would have been the perfect time to be honest with Anne about the thoughts I was having and, maybe in the long run, spare us a lot of trouble, but I lost my nerve.

I got too scared.

Anne had never mentioned how she feels about gay people, but she did always get upset and send vicious looks at anyone who made fun of those kids at school. I used to get really angry with myself for not using this opportunity to come out. Maybe not even technically *come out*, but at least stop hiding these huge feelings inside me. (A lot of guys pretend they don't have feelings. I think that's so stupid. Imagine if we were just honest with ourselves and with the people close to us?)

She would have understood and helped me. I don't think she really ever loved me like that anyway, and I'm positive she would have listened and been there for me until I sorted things out.

But instead, she and I walked away that night as a newly formed couple, unsure of what the future held and just trying to find our way in the world like everyone else.

She talked to her friends that night about things, but I kept quiet. I wasn't unhappy to be with Anne, but I was confused and not necessarily overly enthusiastic. Her friends told my friends, and my three "amigos," Eron, Bailey, and Hunter, barged into my house the next morning...before 8:00.

Or rather, they barged into my window. I was dead asleep until the three of them banged on my bedroom window all at the same time. I said some bad things under my breath but opened the window and they all climbed into my room, being way too loud.

"Be quiet, my family's all asleep!" I hissed at them. "What the heck are you doing here at…" I looked at my phone to see the time. "7:30?"

"Dude, we heard about you and Anne!" Eron punched the air dramatically.

"Yeah, congratulations!" Hunter grabbed my shoulders and shook me back and forth.

Irritated, I asked them again why they were at my house before 8 a.m. on a Saturday morning.

"We stayed up all night," Bailey chimed in. "When Claire and Marjorie called to let us know about you and Anne, it was 3 a.m."

"We at least had the decency to wait until a semi-normal hour!" Eron took a bow.

"What do Claire and Marjorie have to do with anything?" I asked.

Hunter reminded me that they were Anne's two best friends. I asked why the guys had stayed up all night.

"It's been too long since we've pulled an all-nighter!" exclaimed Bailey. "We just played video games all night, and when we realized the sun was coming up, we decided to come crash your house."

"Well, make yourself at home. I'm going back to bed." I turned around and collapsed on the bed, almost immediately falling asleep. If I had been more awake, I would have been in a somber mood because of the guys coming over to "congratulate" me about my new relationship with Anne.

Part of it felt good, that they were so happy for me. But part of me was still conflicted, and I had this lingering notion that maybe I had made a mistake. They knew I had never dated anyone before, so that was probably why this was being made into a big deal. Anne had dated one other person before, but it was in middle school, so I don't think that really counts.

When I woke up a few hours later, the first thing I saw was Eron asleep at the foot of my bed and Hunter on the floor. They were all so comfortable in my house that they had gone to the closets and collected every blanket they could find to make a pallet. I pulled myself out of bed and stumbled into the living room to see Bailey wrapped in a sleeping bag on the couch. His mouth was gaping open, and I laughed.

My parents went to work out every Saturday morning and then have lunch with friends, so the house was still quiet. I fixed myself a bowl of cereal and went outside to eat and think about things before my friends woke up and started causing a ruckus again.

But really, I couldn't think straight. (No pun intended.) I ended up just sitting there and listening to the birds. The sky had some scattered dark clouds.

I heard the door behind me open, and Hunter came out, yawning wide. He had a cup of coffee in his hand, and when he sat down I saw it was nearly white in color.

"Morning," he croaked.

"Since when do you drink coffee?"

"I've always kind of liked it. Trying to use less creamer these days."

I leaned over and took a good look inside his mug. "You've got a lot of work to do, man."

He chuckled and took a sip. "You should see how much I used to put in it."

It felt good to have friends who were close. Even when I felt lost inside myself and confused, and even though I had to conceal a big part of my life, I was still happy to have the guys.

Hunter had this gift of being able to read people's minds, or something like that. Even if he wasn't talking to you, he can still know if something's up. I guess he must have picked up on my vibes, because he cleared his throat and looked at me different than usual.

I knew what was coming.

"You good?"

I think I hesitated literally half a second before saying "Yeah, definitely," because he gave me the I-know-you-better-than-that look.

"Have you ever dated anyone?" I asked.

He took another swig of coffee. "Nah."

"Why not?"

"I don't want to."

"You just want to fool around?" As long as we'd known each other, Hunter and I had never talked about any of this before.

"Nah."

"You don't want to date or fool around?"

"That's right."

"I don't get it."

"There's nothing to get! It's simple."

As two guys who were coming to the end of their teenage years and soon entering college, this made no sense to me. I mean, not that I was an expert on sexuality at this point, considering I was confused about whether I was attracted to guys or girls or both, which should be a pretty simple thing to decide. But with all the pressure and all the casual talk among our friends about sex and dating and relationships, hearing that my friend wasn't interested in any of that was pretty shocking.

"Do you like anyone?"

"I don't want to date anyone."

"Liking someone doesn't mean you have to date them. You can like a million people and never date any of them."

Hunter shook his head. "Nah."

"Are you serious?"

"Yeah, man." He looked at me, and I could see he was serious. "I actually have no attraction to anyone. I honestly can't remember ever being infatuated with someone, just admiring people as friends. Maybe liking someone just a little, here and there. Having a relationship is not on my priority list."

"What is on your priority list?"

"Career, friends, family. I want to get into a good school, so I gotta study like crazy these next couple of years."

"Me too." I was still caught up in what he had said. "Do you ever feel the pressure to date someone?" I didn't mean to ask it; it just slipped out of my mouth. Instantly I regretted it.

"Not really, because I couldn't even if I tried. It's not something that motivates me. I don't want to spend my life alone, but I know that I'll always keep my friends close. I'm sure I'll find someone one day, but I'm not worried about it."

"So what do you do when they talk about girls and all that for hours on end?"

"It's fun to hear them talk about it. They get so frenzied over it, like it's the most important thing in the world or like it makes them more of a man to date all the girls and see how far they can go."

We laughed a little, both imagining all our guy friends together in a big group, laughing and yelling and showing each other pictures of girls on their phones. The more I pictured this scenario, the more I realized I had never really seen Hunter participate in those moments of all the guys trying to out-date each other. I never had really, either, but I had pretended several times.

The guys always labeled me as the secretive one because I would never tell which girl I did what with. Of course, it was all made up.

On nights that I told them I had taken girls to the bridge to see the moon, I had actually stayed home and watched TV or wrote or did homework. I told them a few times I had messed around with girls in the back of their cars, or went out to eat with others, but I had actually gone hiking by myself or run errands for my parents.

Right now, I wanted so badly to tell Hunter all these secrets. Keeping them inside was like poison, but I couldn't bring myself to say the words I so badly wanted to say. Every time I got the courage, I questioned myself again and stayed quiet.

"Why do you ask all these things?" Hunter asked, jolting me out of my trance.

"Oh," I replied, looking at the dark clouds come nearer. "Just wondering."

Chapter 3

"Hey!"

I looked up, startled. The library was supposed to be a quiet place. No one shushed the loud voice that was calling me.

Where are they? I turned in my chair and saw Anne walking toward me from the other end of the room. She was partially hidden by bookshelves. When she emerged, I saw at least 10 books stacked in her arms.

"You need help?" I asked softly, getting up.

"No, I'm fine." She plopped the books down with a loud thud, and someone at another table finally hissed for her to quiet down. A cringe came over her face and she lowered herself into the chair opposite me. "Was I that loud?"

"Yeah." I cringed too, and we covered our mouths as if that would keep us from laughing too loudly. "What are you doing here?"

"I've been doing pretty terrible in history lately and want to bring up my grade," she explained, looking through her pile and holding up a huge textbook with a Baroque painting on the cover. "Miss Ellison said we have to cite our sources MLA, and she wants at least two 'real' books for this paper. I decided to blow her mind and be an overachiever this time!"

"You? An overachiever?" Some of the books had really beautiful covers, and I picked one to look through. Its pages weren't just full of boring words like most other ones. This one had lots of art and paintings and photography in it.

"I know. Surprising, right?" She giggled. It made me smile. I really did like being around her, and I was glad our failed relationship hadn't ruined our friendship. Most of the time it wasn't like that, as I had seen far too many times with the guys' quick turnaround rate for dating.

"By the way, I had no idea I texted you until I got to school." I hoped I wasn't blushing.

"No problem, I could tell you were still pretty out of it anyway." She gave me a little smile before returning to the index of one of the books.

"So…" I wasn't sure if I was being awkward or not. "…why did you text me?"

"Oh, I was just thinking about you on my run this morning. It's been a while since we've talked. Not that I'm trying to steal you from all the other girls! I hear you're quite the ladies' man." With this, she gave me a sultry wink.

I froze, or at least I felt like I did. I hope I didn't freeze in real life. I hope that when she said this, I just smiled and looked normal. To be truthful, I don't really remember what I did, because her comment caught me way off guard. I only remember asking her, "Is that what they all say?"

Anne nodded. "That's what I've heard from some of the guys. It's been a while since they said anything, though. Maybe you've calmed down a bit while getting ready to graduate." At my uncomfortable facial expression, Anne giggled again and reached across the table to gently push my shoulder. "Relax, it's okay. We're cool."

That's not what I'm worried about, I thought so loudly I could almost hear my own voice. "Uh, I'm just gonna study now."

"Did I say something wrong?"

"No, it's…it's fine. I'm fine. Wasn't expecting that, is all."

She frowned. "I'm sorry, Clay."

"Listen, Anne, you didn't say anything. It's fine. Caught me off guard, that's it. You know I'm not a very extroverted person." To lighten the mood, I leaned over the table and whispered in a weird voice, "I get scared sometimes."

She cackled loudly enough for someone else to shush her and slapped her hands over her mouth immediately. "I think I'd better start studying, too, or else I might get kicked out. You I'm not very good at being quiet."

I smiled and returned my focus to my homework. I had a lot to do before tomorrow's class, but Anne's attention motivated me. I enjoyed being around all my guy friends, but it was the quieter ones that I felt closest to, like I could tell them anything (even though I didn't). Not that Hunter and Anne were quiet, but they weren't as rambunctious as the others, like Bailey and Eron. And definitely not as obsessed with people of the opposite sex.

If I were to come out sometime before I graduate, I thought, *I would come out to Anne or Hunter first.*

The thought crossed my mind again that maybe, if I came out, people would tease Anne for dating a gay guy.

I could hear it in my head now: "Anne, that's why you two broke up after less than a month! You wondered why he wouldn't kiss you? Because he's gay!"

Laughter, teasing, more laughter. I wouldn't wish that on her, ever.

Sometimes I tend to think the worst about a situation, and really make people's reactions in my head more terrible than they actually are. I'm almost always wrong about situations, but I feel like I need to be prepared for the worst to happen. My mom used to tell me to lighten up, that all that negativity would bring me down. I can't help it; I try to envision every scenario that could happen in a situation. At least that's better than wallowing in fear all the time.

It took everything in me to not totally freak out at the realization that I might actually be considering coming out before graduation.

Wouldn't that be a great graduation gift to yourself? I thought.

Or it could be the worst, said another voice inside me.

I shook my head to try to dispel the bad thoughts. My heart felt empty; I had just been offered another opportunity to tell Anne, one of my closest friends, the truth, and I didn't do it. She was basically asking me to tell her, even though she didn't know she was!

Because I was in the library, I didn't do anything. If I had been anywhere else, I would have slammed my fist on the table.

That familiar unpleasant feeling of my heart pounding came upon me again, and I took a deep breath. "I'm going to the bathroom," I whispered to Anne, who was fully immersed in her studying. She barely nodded, and I fast-walked to the bathroom.

I need to get some energy out, I decided.

The door to the stairwell was next to the bathroom door, and even though it was only four flights of steps, I climbed them a couple of times until I had broken a little sweat.

My heart was pounding for the right reasons now. I came out of the stairwell and drank a lot of water from the water fountain before going back to the table.

Anne had spread her notebook paper all over the table so I barely had any room to do my homework. Normally I would have stayed, since math homework doesn't take up much room, but seeing Anne made me feel something I couldn't describe.

Emptiness? Loss? Anxiousness? But at the same time, happy.

Either way, I knew I wouldn't be able to get much work done with her there. She was being extremely quiet except for the occasional flipping through the books or pencil scratching on paper, but I was too distracted.

I sat down and began to gather my things, slowly though, so I didn't freak her out. "I'm going to head home," I whispered.

She looked up. "Oh, okay. Finished with your work already?"

"Not quite, just a little left. Dad asked me to go pick up some hamburger buns for dinner, so I gotta go."

"All right. Let's hang out sometime, okay? When we have ten minutes of free time."

"Yeah, sounds good." I smiled and put everything in my backpack, then was gone. The air outside was much less musty than inside the library, and it felt a lot better to be out of there.

Why am I so fragile lately? I wondered. *It seems like everything had been putting me on edge for a while, and I didn't know if something inside me was changing to make me more emotionally fragile or what.*

But maybe I did know what it was. Maybe I really did, at my core, want to stop hiding behind a disguise and start living authentically.

Start living a fuller life that would make me truly happy instead of only sort-of happy.

Start living a life that would make me feel valuable and seen instead of forced to pretend I was someone else.

I thought about how coming out would make me a different person, and I didn't think it would so much. If I came out, I would still be the same person. I would still be Clay. But I would be a lighter, freer Clay who could fulfill his potential.

Because right now, I was a Clay who was preoccupied with this massive burden being carried every day.

I got in the car and started to drive home, feeling oddly confident. It was a strange flip from everything I had just been feeling in the library. Maybe the closed-in rooms made me claustrophobic, but I didn't try to figure it out.

I'm going to come out before graduation. I had to; it was the only choice.

Not only that, it was the right choice. Something that desperately needed to be done.

The longer I waited, the more confused and blue I would get. And maybe in college I would find someone to be with and have to come out to my family with that person. That would be pretty painful.

Yeah. Coming out before graduation is a much better time to do it.

Everyone didn't have to know right from the beginning. I could start with my family, and then leave for college. It wouldn't be such a big deal if I did it that way, right?

Let's hope it goes like that. I sighed. *Now I have to decide when and who to tell first.*

My family deserves to know first, right? Isn't that how it went? I had read probably a hundred coming out stories on the Internet, and every one of them was different. I thought about the ones that were similar to mine.

I have a family, both parents, I go to a good high school, I try to get good grades although I could definitely try harder, and I've got a group of friends who are great.

A lot of the stories I've read start this way, but something was still missing from their lives to make them feel lost. The stories I resonated with particularly well are the ones where the people were from a town and a family like mine, that wasn't really exposed to LGBT things or people. Like, my family had been pretty critical of the LGBT community in the past, and it's amazing how just that one little thing can make me—and the authors of the coming out stories—feel so isolated and misunderstood.

I didn't ask to be gay, and I didn't ask for my sexuality to be such a huge part of my identity. A few times before I'd heard that humans are sexual creatures, which is a scary sounding claim at first, but when I really thought about it, it made total sense. Why else would how we identify sexually play such a strong role in the essence of who we are?

When I drive, I always have lots of good thinking time. Most of my friends just listen to music or call someone to talk. I like talking to my friends, but I also like to have time to think. A crazy thought hit my head once: maybe one day I'll publish all my journals. Everything I think about that I want to explore more, I write about it. For some reason that helps me figure things out more clearly. Writing my thoughts down is a safe place, where I don't have to hide anything. Like I said before, it's not something that 18-year-old guys do very often, but also like I said before, what if people weren't ashamed that they have emotions like normal human beings?

Maybe, if my journals are ever published, they will help teenagers and young adults like me figure things out. Not that I think what I have to say is super unique or special, but I know how good it feels to know you're not the only one experiencing something. Picturing someone who feels alone and dark getting on their feet and being courageous to live their life true to themselves is what keeps me writing.

But here I was, barely able to sit across from my friend because of these fearful thoughts and feelings. *I can't tell any of my friends that I'm gay; I can barely admit it to myself.*

Why not? I took a turn way before I got to my road onto a street that had a huge hill. I rolled all the windows down. Somehow the wind made me feel much better. I sped up the hill and let the car coast all the way down the hill, and I took a breath as deep as I could to refill my lungs with good air.

Because I'm scared of losing people close to me. And if I lose them, I might lose myself.

I knew this was true. It wasn't something I thought, but more like a voice that came into my head and told me what was really going on inside. I appreciated it, but I couldn't handle the pressure anymore.

All of a sudden, I felt like I was going to explode.

I got really lightheaded and my heart did that pounding thing again. Luckily I was close to home, so I took deep breaths and drove home right then. I knew I was driving, but I couldn't see anything.

It was like the world had gone invisible. Nothing existed. I heard my heartbeat in my ear and felt it all the way to my toes. My head began to pound, and my throat got really dry. I started to shake, and I thought I should probably get some of the energy out by running or doing pushups or yelling or something.

But I couldn't make my body move. I had to use two trembling hands to open the door to my house and by that time my skin was numb. The house had that still air about it, so I knew my parents weren't home. I couldn't even manage to wonder where they were.

Somehow I took my shoes off and drank a glass of water. It helped my throat be less dry, but I was still shaking like an earthquake. My legs started to get weak, so I stumbled into my room, crashing into the doorframe on the way.

My body hit the bed and I lay there limply on my side, head twisted so I could stare right at the ceiling. The relief that came with not moving or having to talk to anyone was immense.

As relieving as it was, though, it didn't make the panic attack any better.

It suddenly struck me again like a truck going 100 MPH, and I couldn't keep still. I sat straight up, and my body twitched like I was on a caffeine high. My mind lit on fire, and so much ran through my head at once I couldn't catch a single thought. I stood up and tried to busy myself, stacking papers and opening drawers and rearranging pens like a maniac.

"Clay?"

The voice scared the crap out of me, and I jumped into the air. Whirling around, I saw Hunter standing there, looking really confused. All I could do was nod.

"You...are you all right?"

"Uh..." I tried to tame my tongue and get it out. "Yeah, yeah. I'm okay. Just thinking. I mean, organizing. You know, to get the rest of my homework done." I picked up the first thing I saw, a ballpoint pen, and held it up for Hunter to see.

Instead, he saw how badly I was shaking.

"You're really pale, buddy. What's happening?"

I saw his mouth move after that, but I couldn't hear him for the sound of rushing blood in my ears. I got dizzy and tried to say something, but fell back against the desk. Hunter was beside me in half a second and guided me to the bed.

His mouth moved again, but I didn't understand. He put his hands on my face and looked me right in the eyes. "Do you want some water?" I heard his voice say from what sounded like the distance.

I managed to nod, barely, I think. This attack was like an out of body experience. I couldn't hear or feel myself, or even Hunter. He'd helped me sit down but I couldn't feel his hands on me.

Then, I decided I'd be okay with dying.

"What?"

I looked beside me and Hunter was there, holding a full glass of water. "What?" I whispered.

"Clay, dying isn't something to joke about."

"I didn't say anything about dying." I could barely hear myself speak.

"Yeah, you did. You just said you'd be okay if you died."

"I only thought it."

"No, you said it. You're going to be fine, buddy. Drink some water."

Hunter held the cup to my mouth and made sure I didn't drop it. I felt so useless and empty; I couldn't even take a drink of water by myself? Really?

Slowly, over the next few minutes, I started to feel Hunter's hand on my shoulder. The loud noise in my ears quieted down, and I wasn't shaking as much. I took a big gulp of air and looked at my friend.

"I have panic attacks sometimes, too, especially around final exams," he said, scooting back to lean on the wall. "They can be debilitating."

"This was my first time having one, I think," I said. My voice was rough.

"What happened, buddy?"

I looked in Hunter's eyes and saw so clearly that he cared about me. I felt my eyes get wet, and then a couple of tears dripped down my cheeks.

"I can't keep hiding," I said. "I'm gay."

Chapter 4

"That's what this is about?"

I was kind of dizzy again, but not from anxiety. My secret was out. I nodded, looking at the floor.

"You've been gay this whole time?"

He's angry at me. I've lost him. "I've been figuring it out for a couple of years now, but yeah."

There was a little silence. "So is that why you and Anne broke up?"

"She doesn't know."

"Does Eron know?"

"Nobody knows."

"I'm the only one?"

"Yeah."

"Geez," he muttered to himself. "They kept making fun of the gay kids at school."

"Yeah, they did." I knew he didn't mean for me to answer.

Hunter sat beside me again and looked me in the face. "I have heard of so many people who actually get diseases because they're holding in some major thing that is so important to them, but they are scared to let anyone know."

"For real?" I hoped I didn't have a disease.

"For real."

That makes sense why I keep using the word 'poison' to describe how this feels. At least I felt a little less crazy.

"I can't believe I'm the first person you told."

"I don't expect you to pretend like everything's the same, so I won't be offended if you leave now." I looked back at the floor.

"Are you kidding me, Clay?" Hunter punched my shoulder. It hurt. "Why the heck would I do that?"

"Because…I'm gay."

"So?"

"Things are different now."

"But are they, actually?"

Not to me, I thought.

"I don't think anything is different. I just think the difference is you don't have to keep secrets anymore. Are you gonna let the other guys know?"

Flopping back onto the bed, I pushed a pillow in my face and groaned into it. "I don't know if I will or not. Maybe I just want to lay low until I leave and go to college."

Now his hesitation was a bit uncomfortable. "When are you going to tell your family?"

I looked at him for probably too long, and as a response I yelled into the pillow again.

We were both quiet for a long time, thinking. Well, at least I was thinking, sort of. I didn't really know what to think, except I did feel surprisingly better after telling just one person.

After a little while, Hunter said, "You know, I bet it would change the way the guys make fun of the gay kids if you told them."

"I won't save the world by coming out, Hunter," I replied sharply.

"I'm not saying you will, but you could help them understand it's not okay for them to say that kind of stuff, even behind people's backs."

He has a point.

"It's not good enough to just tell them to stop. They're stubborn."

True.

"If they found out their best friend is gay, that's basically them making fun of you all those times." He stopped. "You know they would never make fun of you like that, right?"

"Yeah, I know." My head was starting to hurt. "I'll be honest, Hunter, I'm really freaked out to tell them."

"I can imagine. But listen, our group, our close group? We've been together for a long time. We've even all seen each other cry at one time or another. Remember when Bailey's grandma died and we all went to the funeral?"

That had been a really sad but kind of funny time. I chuckled, wiping away the remains of one tear lingering on my chin. "Yeah."

"How Bailey was crying and then I started crying and you and Eron started crying?"

We both laughed. "Yeah, I remember," I said.

"Shallow friends don't all cry together like that unless it's a serious bond." Hunter beat his chest with his fist.

Once again, I fixed my eyes on the ceiling. After the panic attack, my body felt more exhausted than it did after a hard workout. "I just don't know if I should tell them first or my family first," I confessed.

Everything I've written in my journal is suddenly coming out to Hunter, I realized. Even though I was steadily growing more and more tired, the feeling of revealing what I had been keeping to myself for several years was exhilarating.

"Who do you want to tell first?"

It was a simple question, but I couldn't decide off the cuff. "I don't know."

"Who do you feel more comfortable telling first?"

"Obviously not my parents." That much was for sure.

"If you ask me," said Hunter, pretending to smoke a cigar like old scholars do, "I think telling the guys first might help you feel more courageous about your parents."

He has another point. "Yeah, maybe."

"What else is on your mind?"

"How do you always know when something is in my mind?" It was kind of frustrating how he could tell so easily.

"I'm psychic, bro!"

"Yeah, yeah, whatever." I waved my hand at him. "What about Anne?"

"What about her?"

How should I say this? "I don't want people to give her a hard time for dating a gay guy."

Hunter chewed his lip. "Me neither, man. But I can't say for sure."

"I just saw her today. She was studying at my table in the library."

"Yeah, she's actually the one who told me you were kind of sad. She parked next to me today and we were leaving at the same time."

"Am I really that much of an open book?"

"Let's just say your face doesn't really conceal what you're feeling very well!"

I wondered how I was supposed to get any homework done when I just made a huge decision to come out to my best friend. What was I supposed to do the rest of the night? Carry on like nothing had ever happened? That seemed completely impossible.

"I'm hungry." Slowly I pushed myself off the bed with a grunt like an old man. Hunter followed me into the kitchen, where we warmed up some leftover pasta from the night before and ate it in silence.

"Where are your parents?"

"I don't know," I said. "Did you tell me you've also had panic attacks before?"

"Yeah, around finals. Especially the essay part." He put a huge bite in his mouth and talked while he chewed. "It's so open, and you never know the mood of the person who will be grading the essays. Multiple choice questions are way more safe."

I dipped my fingers in my water and flicked some on him. He flicked water right back on me. I realized I was smiling just a little and starting to feel better, especially after eating. Food always makes me think clearer.

"I need to talk to the guys," I heard myself say. Clapping my hand over my mouth, Hunter and I stared at each other for a second.

"No problem," he replied.

"I didn't mean to say that," I tried.

"Yes, you did."

"No, I really didn't. I don't know why I said it."

"Because you meant it."

It was true. I knew I was in too deep now. Why did I ever tell Hunter?

Probably because I was having a breakdown and that's a tough one to cover up.

"Don't think about it. Trust yourself."

I took the last bite of pasta and swallowed slowly, feeling it go all the way down to my stomach. Hunter was still looking at me, and without meeting his eyes, I just nodded and began to wash the dishes.

Trust yourself, I repeated. *It'll be okay.*

The guys looked at me with an unreadable stare.

"Have you ever liked any of us?" asked Eron.

"Seriously?" retorted Hunter in my defense.

"It was just a question."

"Just because I'm gay doesn't mean I like every guy in the world," I muttered.

"Yeah, do you like every girl that crosses your path?" Hunter was getting agitated.

"Almost," snapped Eron.

"Even your girl-bros?"

Eron stopped to think. "Maybe not."

"That's what I thought."

"How long have you been gay?" Bailey asked quietly.

I was prepared for this question. "Since I can remember, but I've been figuring it out for a few years now."

"A few years?" yelled Eron. "You didn't tell us for a few years?"

My eyes met the floor.

"Just try to put yourself in Clay's shoes," Hunter intervened. "With something like this, especially with you two mocking the gay kids at school all the time and calling them weird, would you be completely open about it?"

Eron ran his hands through his hair and shook his head. "I don't know, man."

I felt someone staring at me and I looked up. Bailey was giving me a sympathetic look. I could almost hear him: *Don't listen to Eron.*

Hunter stood up and balled his fists. "I can't believe you have to even think about that."

"About what? How this news is totally unexpected?" Eron took a couple of steps toward Hunter.

"Clay is one of our *best friends*, Eron. How can you not be more understanding?"

"He kept this from us for a really long time, *Hunter.*"

"That doesn't matter anything! He's telling us now, and you're lucky he's telling you with how you treat the people at school!"

"Lighten up," I waved my arm at them, feeling a headache coming on. "It's okay, guys."

Eron and Hunter didn't seem to hear me.

"What are you so angry about, anyway?"

"That's a good question, Hunter. I don't know if I'm more angry that Clay's been hiding this little secret for so long without letting us know, or that he's gay at all."

My heart stopped. I never expected to hear such words from Eron.

"Well, supposedly gay, that is," he corrected himself sarcastically and stepped back a little, turning to face me head-on. "Didn't you say you aren't totally sure? Or you weren't sure?"

"I'm sure," I answered before Hunter could open his mouth.

"So what about all those dates you went on? Taking girls sightseeing at night, getting frisky in the back of their cars?"

I didn't reply.

His eyes widened. "Oh, I get it now. That explains why your stint with Anne didn't last very long. You tried to fool around with her and didn't like it, right? So you figured the only logical solution was…"

"With all of your ridiculous conversations about girls, can you blame him?" Hunter interjected. "Most of what you and the guys say is exaggerated anyway."

"Whatever." Eron spit on the ground and looked back at me. "Well, it all makes sense now. The puzzle pieces are coming together. You're positive this is who you are?"

"Non-debatable," I growled.

Eron raised his arms. "There we have it, folks. Our own little fag."

Bailey was suddenly on his feet with his fist grabbing Eron's shirt. He drove Eron's back into a tree behind him and got so close to his face they were almost touching noses.

I saw Bailey's mouth move for what looked like several sentences, but I couldn't hear anything he was saying. He and Eron had a threatening stare-down before he released Eron's shirt.

With a venomous glare, Eron cussed and walked away, got in his car, and drove off.

Hunter and I weren't really sure what to do. We both stood there, open-mouthed. My cheeks felt blazing hot, and I stared at the ground, trying to figure out what was supposed to come next.

"Forget that happened," said Bailey, and stretched his fingers out. One of his knuckles popped. His face was no longer red but had returned to normal. He looked a bit sheepish, but I could see he was also thinking really hard about something.

He walked over to me and put a hand on my shoulder. "Clay, listen."

"It's okay, Bailey."

"No, listen."

I heard in his voice that he was very serious about what he was about to say. I looked him in the eye.

"For all those things you've heard me say about the gay kids and the artsy kids and whoever else, and all the jokes I've made…I'm really, really sorry."

"It's okay." I looked down again.

"It's not okay. I had no idea you were…I mean, if I had known, I would have thought about it a lot harder and never done it." He fidgeted. "No one should say the things I've said about them."

"Bailey," I started.

"Don't say anything. I just want you to know I'm sorry, and that's all."

"Do you think I did the right thing? Telling you and Eron, I mean." My words came out of my mouth faster than I intended.

"Forget about Eron, he's acting like a douche more and more these days. You know he can't stand anyone with a different opinion."

"You, then?"

"If I had gone to college next year and kept making fun of people only to find out way later that my best friend is gay…I'd probably die."

Hunter let out a little laugh.

He was right, after all. Of course.

"I'm hoping that's the same case with my parents," I confessed.

"You haven't told them yet?" Bailey seemed surprised.

"Heck, no. I've lived my whole life hearing them spout their views on gay rights and gay marriage and gays in general. It's not really supportive, what they say." I heard my dad's voice in my head and to get rid of it, I added, "My dad says people are gay to get attention."

Hunter's mouth formed an O shape. "That sucks."

I nodded.

"Well, Eron can get the hell out of here," said Bailey. "We've all known each other basically our whole lives. If we've made it this far, I think we can keep on."

"Have you decided when you're going to tell your family?"

The question made my head hurt even more. "Guess Eron will go blabbing around or something, so everyone will find out soon enough. Maybe I need to tell them tomorrow."

"How about Anne?"

I wished I could say that Anne would be the ultimate coming-out, and it would be easier after that, but I knew it wasn't true. Every time I told someone, it would be the ultimate in that moment. Anne would be almost as hard as telling my parents.

She was my first girlfriend. My only girlfriend. She deserved to know, especially before Eron dared to do anything stupid.

"I'll call her now," I said, and reached for my phone.

Chapter 5

"That's okay."

My head snapped up. "What?"

"I said, that's okay."

The world started to spin. "What's okay?"

Anne rolled her eyes, but it was okay because she was smiling a little. "Clay. You're gay, and that's fine with me."

I had no idea what to say. Finally something came out. "You're supposed to yell and be angry and hit me for screwing up your love life."

"You didn't screw up my love life, silly. I think it's kind of funny."

What's happening right now? I couldn't believe it. This must not be real.

"Eron didn't handle it so well. You'll probably be hearing all kinds of stuff from him."

"I don't care. I never enjoyed being around him anyway."

"Why am I just now finding out everyone's not a fan of Eron?"

"He used to be cool, you know. Sometimes he has flashes of that coolness. But every day he gets closer to graduation, he just gets more annoying." She shooed away an invisible Eron. "Oh well, let him join a frat and party for the next four years! I have my own future to focus on."

"Why are you okay with this?"

She toyed with the bottom of her shirt. "My cousin is gay, and he just came out last year. So I know how important it was for us to keep our cool."

"How were his parents?"

"It took them a while to get used to the idea. He didn't go crazy or anything, he answered any questions they had, and he isn't dating anyone so I think that helps, too." She winked.

"They're fine with it now?"

"Fine as they can be, I guess." She stopped to let me process her cousin's story while she pulled a water bottle out of her bag. "Need a drink?"

I took a long swig and wiped a drop off my mouth. "I think my parents will feel like their relationship with me is going to completely change since I'm gay."

Anne just shook her head.

"No, as in they won't think that?" I was confused.

"I mean, if they do think that, it's not true."

"Yeah," I said, sounding a touch unsure. "Of course."

"Do you really believe that?"

My brain hurt. "I don't know."

"How do you feel now, after telling me? And after telling the guys."

That was something I hadn't stopped to think about. It seemed like a snowball effect—first I had the breakdown that led to me spilling the beans to Hunter, then I told Bailey and Eron at the same time, and now I was telling Anne, all within 24 hours. This wasn't turning out to be a gradual revealing like I had planned it to be.

Well, let's face it; I hadn't really done a whole lot of planning in the first place.

"After telling you and the guys," I repeated, trying to digest the question. "I feel equally relieved and exposed."

She thought about this for a minute, and nodded. "I can understand that."

"I'll probably feel more exposed with my parents, though."

"How come?"

I scratched behind my ear, something I've always done when I'm thinking really hard. "It's just different with parents. Friends are always easier."

Anne took my hand into hers. "Do you want me to go with you?"

I felt really sweaty and nervous. "I don't know if they'll both be home tonight. Maybe Mom has to work…"

Anne didn't buy any of my excuses and held her finger up to my mouth. "Shh. I said, do you want me to go with you?"

I heard myself saying "yes" in a voice that hardly sounded like my own.

Time was frozen. I wished it would stay frozen a little longer.

I looked to my left and saw my parents, Dad sitting in his chair like he did every evening, Mom on the couch with a book on her lap. She had stopped chattering away with Anne.

All three of them were looking at me.

When we had walked in, she wasn't paying any attention to the TV, just enjoying the background noise and the "quality time" spent with my dad.

He wasn't paying any attention to anything besides the TV. The neighbors' cat was howling in our yard, and Mom was letting out little sighs every now and then in exasperation, but Dad was oblivious.

Anne and I had walked in, and I'll never forget their smiles when they saw her next to me. She walked in her usual Anne way over to them and gave them hugs, sitting down on the couch next to my mom and catching up like old friends.

I saw my dad barely notice me, greeting me only with a nod, his sparkling eyes fixated on Anne like she was a daughter who hadn't been home in far too long.

She's setting the stage for me, I realized suddenly, seeing the other empty chair that may as well have had my name on it. *That rascal.*

I stood there for a few minutes, watching the two girls chatting away about any and everything. How they talked so fast about so many things, moving from one subject to another every few seconds it seemed, was beyond me.

Maybe if I were straight I would understand girls more.

Then I thought of my friends who had even less clue about girls than I did. I was practically a knowledge base of women compared to them.

Maybe I understand girls more because I'm not straight.

The thought brought a smile to my face, and I turned away. I was starting to get used to referring to myself as gay, at least in my head. Around other people, that would be a different ballgame, but baby steps.

Don't forget, you're about to come out to your parents in front of your ex-girlfriend.

Just when I had started to ease up, that stupid voice popped back in my head. To be fair, I had almost forgotten for the past few seconds why Anne was at my house.

I guess I had better get ready.

I fixed some water and, after taking a drink, walked over and set the glass down in front of Anne. That's when Mom and Dad figured something was up.

At first they just stopped, Mom mid-sentence, and looked from me to Anne back to me and back to Anne. I saw a tear enter Mom's eye, and I knew what they were thinking.

Before I managed to say anything, Mom asked if we had gotten back together and is Anne pregnant, and I was so overwhelmed I almost let out a laugh because what I had come to tell them was pretty much the opposite of getting Anne pregnant. I thought about how she and I had broken up after I wouldn't kiss her in nearly a month of dating and that's when we realized we just weren't meant to be. I already knew that, after all, but it didn't make it any less difficult.

No, Anne and I said at the same time, and my parents literally took a deep breath of relief at the same time. Anne cleared her throat and nestled back into the couch, and I stiffened.

This is where time froze, and I thought about everything I had spent the last few years processing about myself. All the feelings I had documented in my journal and everything I had held inside me.

It was all about to come out in two simple words.

My vision cleared and I forced my mind to get serious.

They were still staring at me. Anne, not so much. Mom's and Dad's eyes were boring holes through my skull, totally clueless as to what I was about say.

"I'm gay," I said. I didn't know how else to tell them. How exactly to come out was never in the stories I had been reading.

I thought time was still frozen because Mom and Dad held their positions and their stares for what felt to me like eternity. It was only when I saw Anne move her head to look at them then look at me that I knew I wasn't in the twilight zone or some other dimension.

"Well, that's what I wanted to tell you," I finished.

All of a sudden, Mom burst out crying and crumpled down onto her own lap. Anne, without even flinching, reached over and put a hand on her back, rubbing it slowly to soothe her.

I wondered if she had been expecting that kind of reaction.

I looked over at Dad. His eyes had dropped to the floor, and he was focusing very hard on it, almost like he had found some rare and beautiful substance embedded in the carpet.

At this point I had no idea what to do. My dad's eyeballs might as well have been glued to the floor, my mom was on the couch having an emotional breakdown, and my ex-girlfriend was unfazed, as she was examining her nails.

"Why are you here, then?" asked Dad to Anne.

"Moral support," she said simply.

He nodded and looked at Mom. Like she sensed it, she straightened up and took Anne's hand and squeezed it.

"Well," she wiped her nose with her sleeve, something she's never done. Anne handed her the box of tissues sitting on the far arm of the sofa. "On one hand, I'm relieved to hear you're not pregnant."

"Me too," giggled Anne. She and Mom smiled, and I knew Mom was trying to lighten the mood, but her smile was way too sad to be a lighthearted one.

"When did you decide this?" asked Dad.

"I have been trying to figure it out for a few years, whether I really am or not."

"So you've just decided recently?"

"I haven't decided anything, Dad," I replied. "It's not something I decided. For a long time I tried to figure out if I was crazy or not…"

Dad suppressed a laugh that caught in his throat and coughed to hide it. My heart sank, but I kept on.

"…I finally realized I was doing myself more harm than good if I kept ignoring something so important, so I *decided*…" I made sure to emphasize the word so he would get my reference, "…that I was done keeping secrets from the people closest to me."

"If you're gay, why did you two get into a relationship?" The question came so quickly it almost pushed me off the chair.

"Paul," my mom said to him, trying to calm him down.

"It's an innocent question, Suzanne," he retorted. I could tell he was frustrated.

"Clay and I were dating back when he was trying to figure things out. I'm proud of him for trying. He got to know a lot more about himself that has brought him to this point," Anne explained, not leaving them any room to ask more about our past relationship.

"It sure does explain why you've always loved writing," muttered Dad under his breath.

"Paul!" exclaimed Mom angrily.

"What?"

"The fact that I like to write has nothing to do with the people I'm attracted to, Dad." I tried to say it with an even voice but it came out pretty loud.

His eyes went back to that same spot on the floor. "Okay, okay."

"That's a stereotype, you know," I told him defiantly.

"Okay."

Mom started to say something and stopped, thinking before she spoke. She took a tissue and blew her nose. "Have you…?"

"No." She didn't have to finish the question because I knew what she meant.

Unfortunately, I had never met a guy I felt attracted to more than just a friend. I'll admit, I was excited to go to college and meet more people. Maybe I would meet someone there. But these were all thoughts for another time.

"If you don't mind," Dad said, rising to his feet, "I need to go have a think about this. I'll be back in a little while." Without another word, he walked out the back door and started down the sidewalk.

We were all quiet for a little while, just thinking.

Anne encouraged me, "Clay, how about you tell her how you feel."

"I don't want to." Actually, I kind of did, I was just too embarrassed.

"I'd like to know," said Mom, blowing her nose one last time.

Here we go. "To be honest, Mom, I didn't know if I'd be able to do it. Anne helped me so much, so did Hunter and Bailey."

"What about Eron?"

"He…didn't take it well." At my accidental frown, my mom's face dropped. Moms have a sixth sense to know what simple phrases mean.

"Don't worry about Dad. He'll come back to talk to you."

"That's what I'm afraid of," I admitted.

"I'm proud of you, Clay." Anne stood up and checked her phone for the time. "I have to go; I just felt my phone buzz. Mom wants me home soon."

Quickly I stood up. "I'll walk you out. Mom, will you stay here?"

"Sure."

Outside, Anne and I lingered by her car. I didn't know what to say. We had just taken our friendship to a whole new level, I felt. Most friends don't usually sit in while the other one comes out as gay to their parents.

"Thank you for letting me come with you, Clay," she said.

"I should be the one thanking you."

"I have to go, but call me tomorrow, okay? You can even text me tonight if you need me."

"Okay."

"For real, I'm really proud of you. I've just witnessed you taking the first step into the rest of your awesome life." She gave me a smile that was so filled with real joy it made me light up from the inside. I couldn't help but smile back, and I pulled her into a hug.

She kissed my cheek and got in the driver's seat. "Thanks for being my first boyfriend."

"Thanks for being my only girlfriend," I replied, and we both laughed. I watched her drive away and returned inside. Mom was still sitting there.

"She must be really special for you to let her come with you."

"Mom, I've known Anne since I was little. She's one of my best friends."

"She was okay with…this?"

I nodded. "Yeah, she was okay. I've been beating myself up for a really long time about it all, and she helped me feel better about it."

"How about the guys?"

"Hunter and Bailey are great." I pressed my lips together, thinking of Eron's outburst. "I was actually freaking out here and Hunter found me. That's when I told him. And when I told Bailey, he was pretty upset about how he made fun of the gay kids."

"That's funny," Mom said quietly, "because I'm thinking right now of all the things I've said in front of you about…"

"Mom, it's okay. Don't worry about it."

"This isn't something I thought I'd ever experience, if I'm being honest. I need time to process it, but I love you just the same, okay? I'm so glad you feel comfortable telling me. And Dad, too."

Well, that's a change from her initial reaction.

Right then, the door opened and Dad walked in, looking a little fresher than he had before. None of us said anything.

"Anne left?" he asked, sitting down again.

"Yeah, she had to go," I said.

"She all right?"

"She's fine with it all."

"Really?"

"Yeah, she held up better than I did, actually." I wanted him to know how much mental turmoil I had gone through to get to this moment.

"So, how does this change things?"

This question brought back memories of so many hours spent lying in bed on sleepless nights, reading coming out stories from around the world on my phone and wishing I could have my own someday. How many hours had I spent journaling all these feelings that had been boiling inside me, poisoning me, like Hunter had said?

"This doesn't change anything, Dad," I said with a new gentle confidence. "I am exactly the same as I was yesterday. I just don't want to hold in such big secrets anymore. I want to not be ashamed."

He leaned back and crossed his arms, deep in thought. I figured I was getting through to him, at least a little. "I can understand that."

"We are so glad you told us," Mom said again, since last time she had said it he was gone.

"I suppose I'd rather you tell us flat out instead of us finding out the hard way one day when you've found someone," he reasoned, eyes still fixated on something but nothing at all. "What does this mean for the future?"

"Nothing different, really," I said. "Just that one day I'll probably be really happy with a guy instead of a girl."

I had never said these words out loud, and hearing them come from my own mouth sent chills up and down my arms.

I'm okay.

"I'll admit," said Mom, "this is a tough thing to handle, and you certainly didn't let us know gently."

True, I had just come out and said it. There was no gradual build up or anything.

"I don't expect you two to be supportive right now, since it's so unexpected, and especially since you've never come face-to-face with this before."

"Ain't that the truth," said Dad, finally looking me in the eye.

"I only wanted to be honest so one day, when I find someone I love, I can be honest about being really happy and maybe, I hope, you two can be happy for me."

"Honey, I do support you because you're my son," said Mom, some fresh tears trickling down her cheek. She leaned forward and put her hand on my knee. "You have dreams and ambitions and I know you'll excel at whatever you choose to do in life, college and beyond. This is so much more important to me than you falling in love with a certain kind of person."

If I wasn't in front of my parents, I would have let myself shed a few tears, but I had to keep myself in one piece until this conversation was over. Hearing Mom say that felt like a flood of release. Dad unfolded his arms and told me that it would take him a long while to get used to all of this, and he wasn't sure how he felt about it, but he still loved me just the same.

It was pretty late by now. We had said all we could say for the night. I hugged my parents goodnight and went to my room. The first thing I did was get out my notebook and a pen.

Little by little, I'm feeling that terrible burden come off my back. Already I feel ten times lighter than I felt before Hunter found me having the panic attack. It seems like a world ago.

I know it won't be easy in the days ahead, and I know this is only the beginning. But it's a beginning I'm ready to embrace, an adventure I'm ready to embark upon, a story I'm ready to be a part of.

I've only told a few people, but I feel like a new person. Looking back at even just yesterday, I see how holding in such an important part of my identity had affected me so negatively. I never want anyone to hold that kind of mess inside themselves.

Everyone, including me, deserves to live their life freely, not in captivity, and to love who they want to love.

Everyone deserves love, that's a fact, because everyone means something to the world.

If I can use my story to inspire someone to be unashamedly who they are, I consider all of this a success.

And now, I have a life to live.

Invisible (Josh's Story)

"I'm not gay."

I speak these words a little too loudly, and in the small space of the car it sounds as though I shouted them.

"Okay," Ryan says in the driver's seat, staring straight ahead of him at the road. I can tell his body had tensed up. "Sorry."

We're crossing the river, and the length of the bridge stretches out in front of us as the sun sets, casting a golden glow on the surface of the water. The bridge feels impossibly long, like we'll never reach the other side where the bright lights and tall buildings of downtown stand like sentinels, waiting.

We don't say anything else to each other on the rest of the ride home. Twenty minutes of awkward silence. When we finally pull into my driveway and Ryan stops the car, I say a quick "Thanks, see ya later" and get out as quickly as I can. I don't look back as I climb the stairs to my front door and hear Ryan pull out of the driveway and cruise down the street and around the bend.

"How was the movie, honey?" Cindy (my stepmother) asks as I step through the front door. She sits on the couch in front of the TV, already in her pajamas, watching sitcoms.

"Fine," I answer. "Not so scary."

I head down the hall to my room, past my sister's closed door, behind which I can hear her high-pitched giggling, so I know she's talking on the phone to one of her seventeen identical-looking skinny, blonde friends on the cheerleading squad. I get to my room and sit down heavily at my desk, in front of the computer. I switch on the monitor, and my chemistry lab report instantly comes up on the screen, just where I left it, not even halfway done. The cursor blinks at me menacingly. I grab my notebook from my backpack resting at the foot of my bed and open to my notes from yesterday's experiment. There's no way I can get this done tonight, I think. It's already 8:00.

I don't have a choice, really. Either finish the report or watch my already terrible grade sink down even lower.

The car ride flashes across my mind again: an image of the bridge, the river, the lights on the other side. My words echoing as though we were in a cave.

How did this happen? I ask myself. And what do I do now?

Let's back up to a few days ago. Ryan and I are in ceramics class together, the one and only class I have an A in. Mr. Jakowsky calls me "a natural" and "a born artist." He keeps giving me flyers and pamphlets for different art schools across the country and tells me he's happy to help me with my applications next year. I feel kind of bad that I can't match his enthusiasm. All I'm trying to do right now is survive my junior year with my GPA intact. Relatively.

I keep hearing the words of all my other teachers ringing in my head: "You need direction, Joshua"— they always call me Joshua, not Josh, when they try to get serious—"Aren't you thinking about college applications next year?" "This C- isn't going to turn into an A by itself." "You have to try and care more about your work." "I know you can do better than this." I hate that last one. A lot.

But somehow, I've soared through all of my art classes. At the end of freshman year, Mrs. Kerr, my drawing teacher, gave me a flowery card in which she wrote, "I hope you'll continue with your creative endeavors!" She had hung up my best drawing, a self-portrait in charcoal, prominently on the bulletin board, so I had to weirdly see myself looking down at myself every day for the rest of the semester. In photography class sophomore year, my black-and-white photo of a deer that had wandered into our backyard won first place in the art show our school puts on every year. I got a gift certificate to an art supply store, which I still haven't used.

The best way to describe Mr. Jakowsky is eccentric. He wears suits to school that he must have owned since the seventies, and wears glasses as thick as Coke bottle bottoms. His hair is an unruly mass that resembles a huge gray bird's nest. He makes comments on my pieces that I barely understand. Handling one of the vases I made, he exclaimed, "Very Xing dynasty!" He called a pair of candleholders "a neo-expressionist tour de force," and a pot that had developed a wide crack down the side while it was being fired "straight out of de Chirico!" Whatever the hell that means.

I help Mr. Jakowsky run the kiln after school a few days a week, firing pieces made by other students in his classes. Before they go into the loud, blazing furnace, Jakowsky glances over them and usually makes some disparaging comments with a frown on his face. He'll say something like, "Slapdash," or "How elementary," before wandering, befuddled, back into his dusty, cluttered office brimming with art books and haphazardly arranged sculptures balanced precariously on top of stacks of files. Every now and again, in class, we'll hear something topple over in there and crash, followed by Jakowsky shouting, "Damn it to hell!"

Ceramics is the only class Ryan and I share, since he takes mostly upper-level academic classes while I'm stuck in the mainstream. The thing is, it's not that I'm dumb (okay, I am objectively bad at math), but it's that I, as one of my English teachers once so eloquently put it, "lack initiative." I do know—really, I do—that I could do better in my classes if I wanted to. If I really tried. But there's something—I don't know what it is—that stops me, drags me down.

I'd never even spoken to Ryan until he came into the ceramics studio one day after school when I was working the kiln. I was waiting for the pieces to finish firing, sitting at a table still dirty with clay dust, reading The Great Gatsby (or trying to, at least). Thanks to the roar of the kiln, I didn't notice him come in.

"Hey," I heard, and jumped a little in my seat. Ryan was standing right in front of me, across the table. "Sorry," he said. "Didn't mean to scare you."

"It's okay," I said, trying to play it cool. "What's up?"

Underneath the wet, earthy smell of clay that pervaded the studio, I could smell the tang of chlorine. Ryan was on the swim team, and he must've just come from practice. His blond hair, which fell in curls around his ears and grazed the nape of his neck, was still damp, a dark honey color.

"Jakowsky said I could pick up my pot," he said. "It was still cooling yesterday."

"Oh, sure," I replied. "It's probably over there." I pointed to the tall set of metal shelves where the fired pieces are set to cool overnight.

"Cool," he said, and walked over. I looked back down at the pages in front of me, but watched him out of the corner of my eye as he searched the shelves for his pot. Ryan was tall, taller than me, with a broad chest and long, muscular legs. I surreptitiously scanned him over in his white t-shirt, gym shorts, and flip-flops. He spotted his pot on the topmost shelf and reached up to get it, not needing the footstool. The bottom of his shirt lifted up as he reached, almost to his belly button. I could see a faint trail of pale hair leading down to the waistband of his shorts. He took the pot down, and I immediately glued my eyes back on the book, not really reading, and only pretending to look studious.

"Ugh, it's lopsided," he said as he walked back toward me. It was a coil pot, made by coiling a long rope of clay around itself in the shape of a bowl. Ryan's was, well, more than a little lopsided.

"Well, I'm sure Picasso would like it," I said. He looked at me, the expression on his face not one of amusement. "Sorry," I said. Then his face lit up.

"Oh, I get it," he said. "Very funny."

"Can I see it?" I asked. He handed the pot over to me. "Next time, make sure the rope is an even thickness. See how it's thicker here? That why it fell in on itself."

"Great," Ryan said sarcastically. "I'll keep that in mind for when I never have to take a ceramics class again."

I handed the pot back to him. "What's yours look like?" he asked. I pointed to where my pot was on my shelf. He went over to look at it. "Holy shit," he said. "That's amazing. How'd you get those little designs in there?"

I felt myself blush. "I carved them in with a needle."

"Show-off," he said jokingly. I laughed along with him. "Well, thanks," he said. "Gotta go. Um, it's Josh, right?"

"Yeah," I answered.

"Hi Josh. Ryan," he said, and came over to shake my hand. Which, I must say, I found really weird. I mean, we'd gone to the same school for three years, and had a class together for the last four months, and he wanted to shake my hand like he'd just seen me for the first time ever.

I took his hand and shook it. His palms were dry, probably from the chlorine, I guessed. I didn't look at him while I shook his hand.

"Are you a junior?" he asked as he took his hand away.

"Yeah. We haven't had any classes together, though." I thought to myself, *because I'm in the classes for idiots.*

"Cool. Well, see ya," he said and turned to leave. I put my head back down to the book as he walked away, but just as he was about to go through the door, I looked back up. And as he was pushing the door open, he looked back at me at the same time I looked up. Our eyes locked, and he flashed a smile before slipping through the door.

I let out a breath I didn't realize I had been holding. An overwhelming feeling of disappointment washed over me. But disappointment in what? I didn't understand. Was it disappointment in not being able to impress Ryan? To show him that I was somebody, no matter what classes I was in? Then I remembered how I had been watching him from the corner of my eye. How I had become aware of the shape of him, of seeing his bare skin when his shirt lifted up. Of the electric thrill that I tried to ignore as it ran through me when we shook hands.

I wasn't going to pretend that what I felt was anything other than it was. It was attraction. Physical attraction. Ryan was beautiful.

It was like a red-hot poker had been plunged into a pool of ice-cold water inside me. Two extremes meeting: boiling, steaming, hissing. On the one hand, I knew what I felt was real and true. That Ryan was attractive in my eyes. On the other hand, I knew that there was no way to pursue what I felt. That, just like all the other times I had felt some weight inside me tugging me toward another guy, there was nothing that it could result in. Nothing to do about it that wouldn't make me...y'know.

Gay.

I pushed the thoughts out of my mind. The kiln had switched off automatically a while ago, and I put on an apron and huge oven mitts to pull the trays out and set them on the shelves to cool. Once they were all out and the kiln was shut, I swung my bag on my shoulder and prepared to head home. But before I left the room, I stood still, closed my eyes, and listened: the beautiful sparkling sound of glaze cooling and cracking, tiny sharp pops like sparks in space. Miniature starbursts that I could almost see behind my eyelids.

Then, my eyes still closed, an image surfaced in my mind, unbidden: Ryan, his strong, lean arm extended upward, reaching for his pot. The smell of the pool still on him. What it might feel like to lay a hand on his waist, there, just as he stretched upwards...

My eyes snapped open. I could feel something hot and wanting stirring and growing inside me. Quickly, I flicked off the lights, shut the door, and walked down the empty hallway to leave. But no amount of hurrying could cool that heat, and soon, the quick pace of my feet was the result not of my wanting to leave school, but to get home, close the door, and satisfy my body's hunger.

The scent of chlorine lingered on my right hand, the one that shook Ryan's.

Chapter 2

My dad insists that we sit down together once a week, "as a family," to eat dinner. Each of us sits on our own side of the table: Dad, Cindy, Shannon (my sister), and me. A perfectly evenly distributed family. That night, Cindy pulled out all the stops. A pot roast, potatoes, green beans, fresh rolls, corn on the cob. She even lit candles and opened a bottle of wine for her and Dad. Shannon and I came into the dining room, sat down, and gave each other the same look from across the table, supremely weirded out.

Dad also makes us say grace before meals. We have to clasp our hands together and bow our heads, while one of us says the blessing.

"Josh, I think it's your turn," Cindy said.

"No, it's Shannon's. I said grace yesterday," I replied.

"I said grace yesterday, you're such a liar!" Shannon yelled at me.

"Enough, you two," Dad interrupted. "Josh, say grace."

I rolled my eyes as everyone bowed their heads. I saw Shannon smirk at me and resisted the urge to throw a fistful of potatoes at her. "Bless us, God, for this meal we're about to eat," I started. "Bless this food and bless Dad and Cindy and Shannon. And bless me. Especially me."

"Josh," Dad growled.

"Thank you, Lord, for this home, and this food. Thank you. Bless us. You're the man. Amen."

Dad sighed, and we started passing the food around. Cindy and Dad both started talking about their days at work. They both work at the same hospital, Dad as a doctor and Cindy as an accountant. That's where they met, a couple years after Mom died. Shannon and I engaged in our usual zoning-out of the conversation, eating as quickly as we could to get away from the table and back to our rooms. As Dad's and Cindy's voices withdrew into a low hum at the back of my mind, my thoughts wandered to what I had done that day. A calculus test which I expect I bombed. A tooth-pulling discussion of the first few chapters of The Great Gatsby. Volleyball in gym. Working the kiln after school. Ryan in the studio. Ryan talking to me. Ryan shaking my hand…

"Josh? Josh, are you listening to me?" It was Dad, who had apparently been trying to get my attention for some time.

"What?" I asked.

"Did you schedule it yet?" he asked, punctuating the air with his fork.

"What?" I repeated.

"Your SAT?"

My stomach dropped. I was supposed to register for the SAT online, like, last week. I completely forgot. "Oh," was all I could say.

Dad dropped his fork dramatically onto his plate. "Dammit, Josh! Do you have any intention of going to college whatsoever?"

"I'll just take it in the summer, no big deal," I answered, my head down.

"You said the same thing in the fall about taking it in the spring, and now here we are in the spring and you're saying you'll take it in the summer," Dad continued.

Cindy chimed in calmly. "You know, a lot of schools are making standardized tests optional for admission."

"Yeah, which ones?" Dad asked. "Community colleges and safety schools?" Dad went to the Ivy League for college and had put the pressure on Shannon and me to do the same for the past three years. Shannon's going to a good school next year, but not top-top-tier like Dad wanted. So now I get the brunt of all the lecturing.

I try reasoning with him. "Mr. Jakowsky thinks I can get into some good art schools."

"Art school? And get, what, a BFA? You know what that stands for? Bachelor of Fucking Around."

"David!" Cindy yelled from the other side of the table. Shannon snorted, suppressing a laugh.

Angry, I set my fork down, threw my napkin on the table and stood up. "Thanks for your attentive concern for my wellbeing, Dad," I said. "But I don't give a fuck about what you think I should do with my life."

"Josh!" Cindy yelled, at me now. Shannon was dead silent.

I decided to twist the knife. "Mom would've supported me." And I turned and left, walking straight into my room and slamming the door.

Though I couldn't make out any of the words, I could hear all three of them arguing in the dining room. I admit that I felt somewhat guilty about what I said, especially saying it in front of Cindy. There's an unspoken rule that we don't talk too much about Mom in front of Cindy, or compare them in any way. But I was sick to death of Dad pressuring and lecturing me about college, about my grades, about the SAT. He's never seemed to understand why I perform so poorly in school. And, though we don't mention it, my grades began to drop right after Mom died. The thing is, I think Dad expected them to go back up again once we all got over our grief, Dad married Cindy, and we all got on with our lives. But nothing really changed for me.

I took a look at myself in the mirror hanging from the back of my door. Average height, average weight. My father's thick black unruly hair. My mother's square jaw. A body that's easy to go unnoticed. To fade into the background. No close friends outside of school. Not in any sports or clubs. I've felt like I'm just drifting along, one day at a time. Invisible.

But then there's, well...the way I feel about girls. Or don't feel, to be exact. Sure, I had a middle-school girlfriend for a month, but I'm pretty sure every twelve-year-old boy goes through that experience. Once I hit puberty, my attraction to other guys was fully realized. My first few years of high school, I'd purposefully walk past the athletics field on my way home, even though it was in the opposite direction, just to catch a glimpse of soccer or football practice. I had my crushes—tragically unrequited, of course—on boys who I'm sure didn't even know my name. Usually the jocks with whom I shared my classes, as dumb as they were beautiful. Just about every one of them had a girlfriend with whom they would engage in ludicrous public displays of affection in the hallways. I spent my nights fantasizing about what it would be like to be in those girls' positions, muscular arms wrapped around me, lips glued together, tongues dancing wetly inside each other's mouths. Ridiculous dreams that would never come true.

I didn't think these feelings would last. That it was just some kind of weird phase and would, I don't know, just kind of resolve itself on its own. But that wasn't the case. So, was I...what? What was I? I know what other guys would say if they knew how I thought and felt all the time. But that's not who I felt I was. And worst of all, if I were...that...it meant that I would stand out. No longer able to go unnoticed.

The only kids at school I knew who might be gay were part of what was known as the weirdo group. Guys who wore makeup and dyed their hair and girls who held hands and wore t-shirts of bands that no one had ever heard of. That was not me, no way. When I thought of "gay," that's all I could see. No one who was just, like, normal. An average kid.

So I kept it to myself, like I did with most things in my life.

I heard Shannon stomp up the hallway and into her own room, where she, too, slammed the door. Things got quiet, only the sounds of dishes being cleaned up. I knew that we'd all avoid each other for the rest of the night and well into tomorrow. Dad might make some well-intentioned attempt to reconcile with me, and act much more gentler around me for the next few days. But eventually things would go back to the way they were.

I heard a knock on the wall just above the head of my bed. I smiled. Shannon and I had been doing this since we were little kids. Two knocks on the wall that separated our rooms, just to let each other know we were there. I climbed onto my bed and knocked back. We may have grown into complete opposites, but we still cared about each other.

I lay down on the bed and picked up Gatsby from my nightstand to continue the further adventures of Nick Carraway. Who I think was supposed to represent something or other...greed? Innocence? Both? I'm sure I'd know if I paid better attention in class discussion. I just wished there was a movie of the book we could watch in class instead.

Sure enough, the next day went exactly as I predicted. Dad tried to stop me on my way out the door in the morning for a heart-to-heart. I just told him I was going to be late and kept walking.

At the end of the school day, I stopped in Mr. Jakowsky's studio to see if he needed any help with anything. We had a fire drill when we would normally have had ceramics class, so I didn't get to see him that day. When I walked into the room, Mr. Jakowsky was in a precarious position: one arm was in a blue sling, incapacitated, and with the other he was balancing a tray full of clay sculptures, trying to move it from the drying rack to the students' shelves. He could barely hold onto it, and it looked like it would crash to the floor any minute. I ran over to him and grabbed the other side of the tray with both my hands.

"Josh! Just in the nick of time," Mr. Jakowsky said. "Here, help me slide this onto the table." We set the tray down at a workstation.

"What happened to your arm, Mr. Jakowsky?" I asked.

"Well," he said in a high-pitched whine, which I knew signaled that he was in a bad temper. "One of your classmates must have thought it would be hilarious to smear wet clay on the floor outside my office. Naturally, I slipped and went down like the proverbial sack of bricks. According to the medical professionals, I've sprained my wrist."

"Sorry to hear that," I said. "Do you need any help with anything today?"

"Thank you for asking, Josh. There's nothing that needs firing. Just some things need rearranged." He used his good hand to move the sculptures from the tray, one by one, to each student's designated shelf. "Eric Palmer," he said, holding out in front of him what was supposed to be a human head but looked more like a mangled tortoise. "Absolutely no eye for form. Or human anatomy, for that matter." He set poor Eric's piece down, which I'm sure was destined for a C, maybe a C+. "Actually, Josh, now that I think of it, would you do me an enormous favor?"

"Sure," I answered.

"Could you go down into the supply closet for me? I'll give you the key. I desperately need a box of paper towels, but there's no way I'll be able to carry them up here. I'd ask Mr. Delancey, but he's a rather taciturn fellow and, frankly, scares me a bit." I laughed. Mr. Delancey was the head custodian for the school who everyone said still had shell shock from Vietnam.

Mr. Jakowsky handed me his massive key ring that must have held a couple dozen keys. He fingered through it and found the right one. I slipped it off of the ring and pocketed it. "Be right back," I said, and headed out.

The supply closet was in the basement, where the gym and pool are. I headed down the two flights of stairs and down the hallway. I expected the basement to be deserted, but instead there was all kinds of yelling, splashing, and whistleblowing coming from the pool. The scent of chlorine suffused the air, and immediately

I was reminded of Ryan. I wondered if it was the boys' or the girls' team practicing. If it was the boy's…

I took the long way around the basement so I could pass by the pool. A long Plexiglas window took up most of the wall that separated the pool from the hallway, so you could see the whole thing. It was the boy's team. My stomach danced, and I could feel myself getting hot. Twenty or so boys were swimming laps, stretching, or chatting with the coach, all of them in bright blue Speedos, to which my eyes were immediately directed, and then, embarrassed, immediately un-directed. I walked past the window once, a little slowly, making sure not to stare at any of the mostly naked bodies, pretending that I totally didn't care about it. Then I kept walking, circling all the way around the basement floor until I came back to the pool. Just one more time, I thought. Just to see if Ryan…

As soon as I got to the window, there he was, just a few feet away on the other side of the glass. He was laughing, talking with a few of the other guys from the team. He must have just emerged from the pool, because his hair was dripping wet, and a pool of water had formed at his bare feet. His arms were crossed in front of his bare chest, with its little patch of golden fuzz at the sternum, and I could catch the glint of water droplets as they trickled down his smooth stomach toward—

He caught my eye. I couldn't pretend like I didn't see him. We were both caught off guard for a second, but then he smiled, and waved. I waved back. Then his eyes grew wide. He held up a finger. I could hear him say, "Hey, wait!" muffled through the glass, then he waved his hand, motioning toward the door. I stood there dumbfounded, like an idiot who couldn't understand what he was telling me. He pointed again to the door and jogged over to it. I walked over to it, too, wondering what he possibly wanted to talk to me for.

The door opened and a wave of chemically-treated humidity hit me. And in the doorway was Ryan, wet and wearing basically nothing. My mouth went dry.

"Hey," he said, "sorry, glad I caught you." He rested one arm nonchalantly on the doorway, and water dripped from his shoulder down along his ribs. Don't look at his Speedo, don't look at his Speedo, I thought to myself.

"What's up?" I croaked.

"Just thought you should know, Jakowsky gave me a B+ on that pot! You know, the lopsided one."

"Oh, yeah, hey, cool!" I said, a little too excited.

"Yeah, I thought you'd be proud," he said, and flashed a wide grin. Was I crazy, or was that grin...flirtatious?

"Well, great job." A moment of silence passed between us. I felt the need to fill it. "So, uh...swim practice?"

"Oh, yeah," Ryan said. "Trying to work on my breaststroke."

"Cool," I replied. I had no idea what to say, knowing absolutely nothing about swimming whatsoever.

"Not really," Ryan said, and we both laughed. "The main reason I swim is so that I can—" he continued, but didn't finish his sentence. "Um." What was he trying to say? An embarrassed look crossed his face. Quickly, he changed subjects. "So what're you doing down here?"

"Oh, Jakowsky sprained his wrist and asked me to get a box of paper towels for him out of the supply closet," I explained, pulling the key out of my pocket to show him.

"Hey, teacher's pet," Ryan laughed. "Lemme know if there's anything good in there. I hear Delancey stashes his coke with the old history textbooks." We both laughed.

"Sure, I'll let you know," I said.

"Well, see ya, Josh," Ryan said, waving.

"See ya," I said, and walked down the hall and around the corner. I stopped there, wondering about our conversation.

It was admittedly strange that Ryan stopped me to talk. And about what, anyway? Did he really have to tell me that he got a B+? And did he have to tell me while he was wearing a Speedo and dripping wet? But then I began to second guess myself. He's just being nice, I thought to myself, friendly. That's what people do. Was I truly that insecure in my self-worth that I had to puzzle out why someone would even speak to me?

I used Jakowsky's key to open the supply closet and flicked on the fluorescent light inside. It was like a short hallway, lined on either side with metal shelves and filled with cardboard boxes. While I pushed aside cleaning supplies as I tried to locate the paper towels, I thought of that strange pause in our conversation, as though Ryan were stopping himself from saying something to me. What was it he was trying to say? Visions of his tall, strong body danced in my head, the smell of chlorine still in my nostrils, a smell I now associated with Ryan and, weirdly, prompted some unannounced stirrings below my belt. I wondered about Ryan changing back into his street clothes, pulling down the rubbery Speedo, rubbing himself dry with a towel...

No longer paying attention to what I was doing, I knocked into a shelf and a large box fell right onto my head. Painfully startled out of my steamy reverie, I looked down and saw that it was, in fact, a box of paper towels. I pushed it along the floor and out the door with my foot, closing and locking the door of the closet behind me. I couldn't hear anything coming from the direction of the pool, so I figured practice was over for the day. But just in case, I walked to the staircase from the other direction, so I wouldn't pass by again. More importantly, I held the box out in front of me, hiding the general area of my crotch. Visions of Speedos still danced in my head, and I hoped that by the time I got back to Jakowsky's studio, I'd be able to put the box down without the risk of it looking as though something was trying to burst out of the zipper of my jeans.

Chapter 3

I spent that night successfully avoiding any interaction with my family, instead trying in vain to pull together a decent report on The Great Gatsby. As it turns out, there is a movie of the book, and no, we're not watching it in class, according to Mr. Philips. "If you want to know what happens in the book," he said, "read it."

I ran into Ryan again the very next day, this time in the hallway right before lunch. I was at my locker, swapping out my textbooks, when I heard him say, "Hey, Josh," behind me. My heart jumped—why did it always seem to do that when he was around?—and I turned to see him smiling next to me.

"Hey, Ryan," I said. "Nice hair." He'd clearly gotten a haircut yesterday, it must've been after practice. The sides were buzzed short and the top was trimmed, but still long enough so that his curls bounced beautifully.

"Thanks," Ryan laughed. "Coach made me do it. Said my hair was slowing me down. I guess this makes me more aerodynamic or something," he said, raking his fingers through his hair. I thought about what it would feel like if I raked my fingers through his hair. Then, he did something I was not prepared for. He reached out and ruffled my hair. "We kinda match," he said. It was true, my hair was cut similarly, and I had a mass of thick and wavy hair on top that was immensely difficult to tame.

"Watch it," I joked. "It takes hours to get that just right in the morning."

"Sorry!" Ryan said through an even wider smile. Then something caught his attention. He was looking at a picture I had printed out from the Internet and taped to the back of my locker door.

"Is that Laura Palmer?" he asked.

"You've seen Twin Peaks?" I asked back.

"Yeah! That's so cool that you have her picture there. I don't think many people would get who it is."

"You're the only person who has so far."

Ryan looked at me, thinking. It was kind of unnerving, having him just stare at me like that. "Do you like horror movies?" he asked. "Like, good ones. Not that shitty Paranormal Activity crap."

"Yeah," I said. "I really do." It was true. I was kind of a horror movie nerd, much to the chagrin of the rest of the family. But by now they had gotten used to the sound of Theremin music and high-pitched screaming blaring from my computer speakers in my room.

"Did you see that new movie about the cannibal family?" he asked.

"Feed? No, not yet. I really want to, though."

"Wanna go see it some time?" His question came quickly, and his facial expression betrayed a hint of uncertainty right after the words left his mouth.

I was determined not to let any awkward pauses enter into the conversation. I didn't even let myself think about responding, I just did. "Yeah, sure!"

The bell rang, and I realized we were alone in the hallway and should've been in the cafeteria by now. "Cool, should we exchange numbers?" he asked, pulling his phone from his pocket.

"Sure," I answered, and we swapped phone numbers.

"Okay, I'll text you," he said.

"Sounds good," I answered, closing my locker.

"See ya!" he said and walked away.

I didn't know what I felt more confused about: the fact that I had never really "gone out" with friends before, let alone get anyone's phone number, or the fact that, of all people, it was Ryan who was planning to hang out with me. I have Ryan's phone number. But then I wondered why he even wanted to hang out with me in the first place. We lived in completely different worlds. He hung out with the smart kids and the athletes. I hung out with nobody. He was tall and handsome, I was, well, at least average, or so I liked to think. Another part of me said not to even think about it. Just enjoy the fact that someone this nice and this hot is paying attention to you. Wants to be your friend.

Jesus, I thought, what if he knew how many times he's given me a hard-on.

I shoved these thoughts aside and rushed to the cafeteria, hoping that I'd make it before they ran out of lasagna.

That evening, I got a text.

Hey, it's Ryan

I texted back: *Hey, what's up*

Movie saturday?

Sure. I felt the need to follow that up with something more substantial. *Where at?*

How about the new Cinemark? I had heard about this one. Supposedly all the theaters had recliners in them. Now Americans were too lazy to even stay seated upright while watching a movie, apparently.

Cool. A few minutes went by. I felt like I needed to say something else, but then my phone buzzed again.

I have a car. I can pick u up. Check out the times let me know which is best

OK i'll let you know

Ryan sent back a thumbs-up emoji. I must've swiped through the emoji list five times before finally deciding on the right one to send back: scared face exhaling a ghost. It felt appropriate.

Ryan replied with a *Lol.* Today's teenagers have such deep conversations.

He did indeed have a car, a red Honda Civic, which he referred to as his "Mom car." We had settled on the 5:00 showing, and I looked forward to a seventeen-year-old's dream dinner of buttered popcorn and Reese's Pieces. Dad was still at work when Ryan pulled up to our house, but Cindy was home, and I told her I was going to see a movie with a friend.

"You're doing what with who?" she asked, trying and failing to hide her incredulity.

"Seeing a movie. Feed. With a friend. Ryan. He's here. We're driving to the Cinemark."

"Oh. Okay. So you won't be home for dinner?"

"No, sorry. Should be back around eight."

"Okay, well. Have fun!" Cindy said, overly cheerful. I could tell she was both worried and excited by the fact that I was going out in the evening with a friend, something I'd never done. Worried that no one had ever met this person, so he could be anyone, even a drug dealer. And excited because it seemed I was finally making an effort to come out of my shell and be more sociable.

I half-expected Ryan to show up with a few more people in the car, ready to be disappointed that we weren't actually going to be alone, that I had totally misunderstood the situation. But no, the car was empty, and I slid into the passenger seat. I didn't yet have my license and felt a little childish being driven around, especially by a guy I had the hots for.

Our suburban neighborhood was on one side of the city, and the new multiplex was on the other. We took the highway around downtown, watching the tall steel and glass buildings pass by, the parks with their statues and fountains. "I have to get into the city more often,"

Ryan said. "Sometimes I feel like I'm going insane in that suburb."

"I know what you mean," I replied. "My family used to come down to the museum a lot in the summers. Back when my mom was…" I trailed off.

"Are your parents…together?" Ryan asked. This being the twenty-first century, it's a fifty-fifty chance that any given kid's parents are separated or divorced.

"My mom died when I was twelve. My dad's remarried, though." I really, really didn't want to bring up my dead mom with Ryan, but there it was, slipped out of my stupid mouth.

"I'm sorry," Ryan said. There was a bit of silence as we continued to drive. I desperately wanted to change the subject.

"How much do I owe you for the tickets?" I asked.

"How about you just buy the popcorn for us?" he said. "It's probably just as expensive." We both laughed.

"True," I replied. "So, don't you have, like, jock friends to hang out with tonight? No offense."

Ryan smiled. "Have you met the guys on the swim team? They're so obnoxious. I try to spend as little time with them as possible. I just consider myself lucky I get to watch them splash around in their little loincloths every week."

I tensed up, immediately. Was that a joke? I thought to myself. He's joking. Yeah. I mean, swimming is pretty…homoerotic. Haha. Funny. I laughed, hoping that was the correct response, before once again playing the change-the-subject card. "So, where's the movie theater?"

It was part of one of those big suburban shopping and entertainment complexes, huge and hulking in the middle of an asphalt prairie between a home improvement supercenter and a pet supplies store. We picked up our tickets and navigated through the mass of children, arcade games, tired parents, and couples on dates. Ryan went to the bathroom while I waited at the concessions counter for a bucket of popcorn and a few bags of chocolate.

The theatre was indeed one of those new ones with what appeared to be automated pleather La-Z-Boys instead of actual seats. Ryan and I settled into ours and giggled as we fidgeted with the controls, the chairs squeaking as they reclined. I set the popcorn on the armrest between us. As is usually the case with these things, we couldn't stop ourselves from eating a third of the way through the bucket before the previews had even ended, which mostly advertised remakes of action movies from the eighties and more summer blockbuster horror movies. "Isn't that, like, the eighth film in that series?" Ryan whispered. He leaned over close toward me so I could hear, and I felt his breath warm against my cheek. I turned to answer and found his face a few inches from mine. We both moved our heads back, a little startled at how close they were, and settled back in our seats as the movie began.

The movie ended up being not half-bad. A family tradition of cannibalism, an isolated house in the woods, intimations of black magic, that kind of thing.

Ryan and I had managed to finish the gallon of popcorn halfway through the film and set the empty bucket on the floor. There was a moment near the end of the film when the hero, by this time pretty decently covered in blood, was picking a lock, trying to get into the basement of the house to release the humans that were caged up down there, being fattened in preparation for consumption. The deranged grandmother, however, had snuck up behind him and suddenly attacked. You could feel the audience—myself included—jump in their seats. Ryan reached a hand out and clutched at my wrist. I laughed, thinking that he was trying to scare me even more, but he left his hand lingering there for minutes, until the scene was finished. A warm feeling spread through me, having his hand there against the skin of my wrist. I glanced over at him, but his eyes were glued to the screen. The light played on the features of his face. I thought about how easily I could just lean over and plant a kiss on his lips, right then and there...

Then, someone in the film fired a shotgun, the audience jumped again, and Ryan snatched his hand away.

We both agreed that it was a good movie, but could've been scarier, and the end was a little disappointing. We made our way out and back to the parking lot, squinting at the low sun shining in our eyes. "I feel like a cave troll whenever I walk out of a movie theatre," Ryan said.

We chatted about the movie on the car ride back, comparing it to other ones we've watched, discussing the classics like Carrie and The Exorcist. There was a slight lull in the conversation as we approached the bridge over the river, heading back across town.

Ryan said, "Thanks for hanging out. You're a pretty cool kid, Josh," and gave me a friendly soft punch on the shoulder.

"Thanks. You too," I said. "Just keep your hands on the wheel."

I could tell Ryan was nervous about something. Which was weird, because I was supposed to be the nervous one here. "It's, um, hard," he said. "To find nice guys." He paused again. "To go out with."

That's when it hit me. I felt cold and hot at the same time. Every muscle in my body clenched. This was a date, I thought. We just went on a date, and I had no idea.

I panicked. There was no way this was happening. This shouldn't have happened. This was a mistake. I knew I shouldn't have gone out. That there was something off about Ryan being so friendly with me. But I had no clue that he was, well, I guess…

"I'm not gay," I blurted out.

I think you know the rest, dear reader. We've come full circle. "Okay," Ryan said softly. "Sorry."

Then, the silent car ride home. Back in my room, the unanswered question still in my head.

What now?

Chapter 4

Knock knock. Two taps on the wall above my headboard.

I turn my head and look at the clock. 2:05 a.m. Why is Shannon knocking so late?

I knock back. She didn't wake me up. I was barely sleeping, more like dozing in and out of semi-wakefulness, replaying the events of the last few days in my head.

Now the knocks are at my bedroom door. I get up to open it, and there's Shannon in her pajamas.

"Hey," she says, "sorry if I woke you up."

"I wasn't sleeping," I answer, albeit groggily. "What's up?"

"Can I come in?"

"Yeah, sure." I open the door wider and Shannon comes in and sits down at the foot of my bed.

"Oh my God, it's a mess in here. And it smells like boy."

"Well, I'm not sure why you're surprised about that," I say, sitting down next to her. "Everything okay?"

"Couldn't sleep," she says. "And I haven't seen you for days."

"We live in the same house, Shannon, of course you've seen me."

"Yeah, creeping around corners and behind closed doors like a freaking vampire or something. You watch too many weird movies."

"I've just been feeling...weird, I guess."

Shannon pauses a second before saying, "You know, you really hurt Dad and Cindy's feelings the other day. When you brought up Mom. That wasn't right."

"I know," I say. "I just remember, near the end, when all she could do was lie in bed, I kept drawing her pictures, remember?"

Shannon smiles. "Yeah. Dragons and knights. You were obsessed with Lord of the Rings. They were pretty good."

"And Mom always said to me, 'These are beautiful, Joshy. You're an artist. Don't ever stop.'"

"She did?" Shannon asks. "I didn't know that."

"And Dad's always being such a dick about college."

"Well, yeah, honestly, he is," Shannon says, and laughs a little. "I think that because I'm not going to the college he wanted me to go to, he's kinda placing all his hopes on you. And let's face it, you're kinda hopeless right now."

I know Shannon meant it as a joke, but something in what she said stings to the core. Maybe it was from the lack of sleep, or emotional confusion, or a bit of both, but I feel hot tears welling up in my eyes. I blink and they fall down my cheeks.

"Oh my God, Josh, I'm sorry, you know I didn't mean it," Shannon says.

"No, I know," I say, my throat constricted. "It's just...it's been a shitty few days."

"I'm sorry, Josh." I wipe my eyes. "But Cindy said you went out with a friend today. That's good. You need to get out more. Experience some daylight."

I heave out a sigh. "Shannon," I start, "I need to tell you something, but you can't tell a soul, okay?"

"Sure," Shannon says, "pinky promise," and she locks her pinky around mine like we used to do when we were little.

"My friend, Ryan," I say, "we went to see a movie. That cannibal one."

"Ugh, gross," Shannon says.

"But...Ryan...he's nice. But." I don't know how to say it. "I think...he thought it was a date."

"Oh my God," Shannon says, and laughs. I don't. "Oh, c'mon, Josh. That's kinda funny. You were that oblivious?"

"I guess," I answer, and don't say anything else.

"That's it?" Shannon says. "Josh, that's not a big deal. It was an honest mistake on his part, I'm sure." I remain silent.

"Josh?" Shannon says, touching my hand. She swallows. "Josh, did you, like, want it to be a date?" And I can feel more tears start to well up, my bottom lip trembling.

"Oh, Josh," Shannon says, and wraps me in her arms while I cry for a long time. "I love you, Josh," she says. "You're okay. I know high school sucks. And I'm sure this sucks. I don't know what you're feeling. But you're my brother. And nothing will change that."

I wipe my eyes and nose on my t-shirt. "Gross, Josh, get a tissue," Shannon says.

"Thank you, Shannon. I love you too," and I grab for her t-shirt to pretend to wipe my nose on it, while she pushes me away.

We laugh and just sit for a while. "So," Shannon says, "does this mean we get to talk about cute boys together?"

"Maybe," I answer, smiling. "But there's only one cute boy I'm able to think about right now."

"So, what are you going to do?" she asks. "You're gonna talk to him, right?"

"I guess I have to."

Shannon pats my back. "You'll be fine. And you know, I'm not saying anything to anyone, not Dad, or Cindy. But, when the time comes, and you're ready to talk to them, let me know. I want to be there with you, too. Okay?"

"Okay," I say, and wrap my pinky around hers. "Pinky promise."

I knew there was swim practice after school on Monday. I decided I'd try to grab Ryan as he left so we could talk. Though I could've texted him over the weekend, I couldn't bring myself to do it. I needed time to process things, figure out what I wanted to do. Since talking with my sister—no, I need to start calling it what it was—since coming out to my sister, I'd been feeling a lot better about things, like I could breathe easier. I even woke up early on Sunday and made pancakes for everyone, causing my family to check to make sure that I wasn't an alien body snatcher who was only taking the form of Josh.

It's hard, almost impossible, to focus in school. I keep thinking that I've spotted Ryan in the hallway everywhere I go, but I never see him. We don't have ceramics on Mondays, so there's no chance of seeing him in class, either. I'll just have to wait. I fidget with just about everything I can get my hands on, including the change in my pocket, which is when I realize that I still have Jakowsky's key to the supply closet. I must've forgotten to give it back, and he hasn't noticed. I briefly consider all the opportunities I have now to swipe some single-ply toilet paper, but try not to let the power get to my head.

Finally, school lets out. But I still have some waiting to do. Swim practice will last for a couple more hours, and I need to catch Ryan before he leaves. I decide to use the time to finish reading The Great Gatsby, which I was supposed to do last week. I go outside and sit on a bench near the door that lets out from the gym, where I figure the team will leave from at the end of the day.

It turns out that trying to finish the book is a terrible idea in this state of mind. The words just swim on the page, and I barely manage to make it through a single chapter. I check my watch every two minutes. Finally, the door swings open, and some of the guys on the team start to come out, duffel bags slung on their shoulders. I try to remain discreet, keep my eyes on the book, but continue to dart my head toward the door every time it opens. Then, at last, Ryan comes out, alone. I shove the book in my bag and stand up. He sees me, and stops. I wave, shyly, and a mix of gladness and confusion crosses his face. I gesture him toward me.

"Are you waiting for me?" he asks as he walks up to me.

"Yeah," I say, feeling myself blush.

"Have you been waiting since school ended?"

"Yeah."

"Okay."

I take a deep breath. "I wanted to apologize. For what I said. Did. The other day."

Ryan looks at me, brows slightly furrowed. "Okay," he says. I can tell he's expecting me to say more.

"It was really cool of you to hang out with me. I had a great time." Even though I rehearsed what I was going to say, I'm still nervous and trip over my words. "What I mean is...I guess, maybe, you thought we were, like, going out, or something." *Beautifully articulated, Josh, you moron*, I think to myself.

Ryan's eyes cast downward, and I can tell he's embarrassed. "Well, kind of," he admits quietly.

"Do you mind if I ask," I begin, "I mean, are you...gay?"

Ryan looks back up and into my eyes. The late afternoon sun catches the brilliant blue of his own eyes, and I see past my own embarrassment, shame, and confusion, and remember how much of a crush I have on him.

"I don't talk about it, really," he says. "But yes. I mean, I know I am. I'm sure of it. But I just haven't, y'know. Come out."

"So," I say, "did you think that I am, too?"

"It's hard to explain," Ryan says. "Sometimes you just get a vibe from someone. You can see it in their eyes when you talk to them. It makes them look kind of lonely, I guess. But also excited. And I thought I saw that in you." He flashes a smile. "Sorry. I guess my gaydar was way off."

"No, Ryan," I say, "it wasn't."

He looks confused. "But you told me, in the car, you said you're not gay."

"I was scared. I was scared of the fact that someone liked me. And that I liked them back. I haven't really come to terms with it myself. So I freaked. And I'm sorry for that."

Ryan's smile grows wider. "It's okay, Josh," he says. "I understand. Completely."

We stand there for a while, just smiling. I can feel the magnetism between us, pulling us closer together.

"So you like me, huh?" Ryan says.

I laugh. "Yeah, I guess I do," I answer. "But I didn't realize just how much till I saw you in your Speedo."

A tomato-red blush rises to Ryan's cheeks, and he laughs loudly. "I'm not gonna lie, Josh, I kinda wanted to talk to you while I was in my swim gear on purpose."

Now it was my turn to blush. "Hey, remember when

we were talking, and I kinda stopped myself in the middle of a sentence?"

"Yeah, I do."

"Well, what I was going to say was, the only reason I swim is so that I can hang around a bunch of cute guys in their wet underpants." We both burst out laughing. "The problem is, it's a little difficult to hide anything if you get too excited."

So this is what flirting's like.

I put my hand in my pocket, and when I feel what's in it, an idea springs to mind. "Is that door unlocked?" I ask.

Ryan turns around. "The one back into the gym? Yeah, why?"

"C'mon," I say, and tug him by the hand back inside. The basement is empty, and we walk past the pool and around the corner to the supply closet. "Look what I still have," I say, pulling the key from my pocket.

"Um, okay," Ryan says. "Do you need Lysol or something?"

I unlock and open the door, flick on the light, pull Ryan inside and shut the door behind us.

"Jesus, Josh," Ryan says, "we're literally in the closet. Whoa, I didn't realize how big it is in here. It's like the size of a classroom. I wonder if they keep the—"

"Shut up, Ryan," I say, grabbing the front of his shirt and pulling him toward me, kissing him hard and insistently. I can feel both of our hearts beating as fast as if we're swimming a race. And I am swimming, swimming in the joy of this moment, in the heat of his lips on mine, in the feeling of shock in Ryan's body that softens and gives way, as he kisses back, takes my face in his hands, both our mouths parting, my fingers twine through his hair, and we're all lips and tongue and breath until we part, gasping.

We both look at each other, holding each other. The smell of chlorine on his skin now lingers on mine. "So, when do you think Mr. Delancey's gonna pop in here looking for his coke and catch us?" Ryan asks.

"I don't care," I say, and bring myself toward him again, needing to stand on my tiptoes to reach, as we both wrap our arms around each other's waists, pressing against each other, into each other, eager, wanting.

A half hour later, we finally come out. Go ahead, make all the "coming out of the closet" jokes you want. But for those thirty minutes, that closet was the only place I wanted to be.

My final project that year in Mr. Jakowsky's class was a ceramic bust of my mother. I based it off of a picture I took of her that I keep framed in my room. It's from before she got sick, a perfect portrait in which she's alive and beautiful. Mr. Jakowsky, with my permission, submitted it to a national competition for young artists. It's been selected as a semi-finalist, and I get to travel to the final award ceremony next month, all expenses paid.

When my dad saw the bust I made, he cried. I'd never seen him do that since Mom's funeral. He hugged me and told me how proud he was, and how sorry he was that he had been pressuring me so much about college. I promised him I'd try extra hard to keep my grades up if he'd support me when I applied to art school. He agreed.

Soon after, Dad and Cindy and I sat down for that talk. Shannon, of course, was there, too. This time, it was Cindy's turn to hug me and cry, tell me how proud she was. Since then, she and I have grown a lot closer.

Ryan's been going through the process of coming out, too. We've both agreed to keep things pretty private in school, until next year, when it'll probably be easier once we're seniors. I guess you could say we're "going out," but it's not like we're having candlelit dinners in French restaurants or anything. We're teenagers, after all. Our idea of a date is getting pizza and sending Snapchats back and forth to each other.

For once, now, I look forward to school. I look forward to waking up and working on my artwork. I finally spent that gift certificate to the art supply store and set up a drawing desk in my room, and even built a darkroom in the basement. I don't feel like I'm floating along anymore. I've stopped trying to blend into the background. I've stopped wanting to be invisible.

Oh, and one more thing. Jakowsky's never realized that I didn't give him the key to the supply closet back. So I still wait for Ryan after practice every Monday, jiggling the key in my pocket, anxious and eager.

We've gotten really good at making out without knocking over any brooms.

After the Football Practice (Grant's Story)

Well, I don't exactly love writing, but I know how to make at least some sense when I write, and I know what I want to say here. So here it goes.

This is a pretty important story for me to share, because it's changed who I am so much.

A year ago, I was newly seventeen and was a completely different person. I was pretty jaded and thought I ruled the world, and that everything would always go according to my plan. It was just me, myself, and I.

I thought I could get away with anything just because I'm great at football, and I have cool plans for my future, and I'm not the worst looking guy in the world.

But from where I am now, I realize that I had a lot of inner turmoil that caused me a lot of confusion and pain.

At the time, a year ago, I thought I was surrounded by friends who were really awesome people. I didn't necessarily think I'd be friends with them forever, because I know from my older brother's experience in college that you end up staying in touch with only a couple of people from high school.

But I thought that at least they were good friends to have while I was still in school. I hung out with my friends a lot, did things we probably shouldn't have done with them (no regrets!)…the usual stuff high schoolers do.

I'm the running back on the football team, and I have been since sophomore year. The only year I've ever not played was freshman year, and I didn't feel myself the whole year because of it. I started playing football at the youngest age you can start, and I've been in love with it ever since.

Several of the guys I hung out with the most were also on the team; that's how it usually is. Teams stick together, and it's not a huge school we go to. Pretty good size, but not the largest school in Boston, probably because we're not in the main city. That's what I guess, at least.

So, unless you just really hate each other or your schedules conflict, there's not much room to avoid hanging out with each other.

Which is cool. I like lots of different kinds of people hanging out together. I like to see how different everyone is. You could call it a hobby. I'm not sure if it goes in the "people-watching" category or not, but it's something like that.

A year ago, that was my simple life, hanging out with people, watching what they do, going to school, and, if we're honest, not trying very hard to make good grades, because I was preoccupied with having already gotten a football scholarship to college.

And taking up even more of my time: waking up too early to practice, working out in the evenings, and keeping up with every football game being played around the country.

I wanted to be the best. (I still do.)

Then some things happened, which I'll talk about later, that were a blow to reality for me, and I had to grow up in some ways I didn't think I'd have to.

When all this happened, I felt pretty alone, because sometimes the people you expect would be there for you in tough times aren't there.

The only people I had to turn to were my two older brothers and my younger sister. But especially my oldest brother, Jake.

I'm writing this because I don't want anyone to feel alone like I did. There's a big community of people out there in the world to accept anyone who feels alone. No one is ever truly alone. Sometimes you just have to work with what you've got, or keep going for a little while before you find someone who really understands what's going on with you.

That much I'm confident about.

The details: I'm gay.

You already knew that. After all, that's why I'm writing this.

I know, most people are surprised to hear that I'm a jock and I eat, breathe, and live for football (other sports, too, but football is the best in my opinion). And I get it, it's not super common to have gay guys, or at least gay guys who are out, in positions like I'm in.

But, of course, that's just a stereotype. I've heard it a million times. It doesn't bother me anymore. When I first came out, it did make me self-conscious sometimes, but I realized I shouldn't let that bring me down since it's not true.

I would say I'm close to my siblings and that we have a good relationship. We never hold grudges (for too long). We get upset with each other at least a few times a week, but it goes away pretty fast, and we just keep going as we were.

The three of them have known I'm gay for a long time. I didn't talk to them about it very much, and most of the time they respected my privacy. But sometimes they teased me about it at home. On occasion in front of my parents, but my parents never responded. They just kind of ignored it. In fact, they never said anything to me about it until I officially came out to them. I'm not sure they ever thought it was serious, you know how people make "that's so gay" and "you're gay" jokes, which is what most of the teasing actually was.

The reason my siblings have known for a long time is because when I was younger (around twelve), we were looking for a house to live in. While my parents were searching, my whole family lived with my grandparents in their big house.

My siblings and I shared the big basement, which was fun because we had four mattresses lined up and had pillow fights almost every night. My parents were upstairs in the extra bedroom, out of earshot.

I think it's definitely a sibling thing to talk about all kinds of stuff you can't talk about in front of your parents when you're away from them and know they can't hear you.

(But we did look around for a baby monitor to make sure they weren't listening. Yeah, we were paranoid.)

At one point in the night the conversation topic always went to who we thought was cute, and my oldest brother, Jake, would always talk about some girl who was in high school that was falling in love with him, and he would brag because apparently having an older girl fall for you is something major. (She probably didn't even exist.)

My second older brother, Isaac, would name some girl in his class that he thought was pretty, but they didn't do anything for him at the time. He didn't start actually liking girls until he was well into high school. He was a late bloomer and still admits to it.

My younger sister, Carol, always talked about which boys on her favorite kids' TV shows were "sooooo cute" and "had happy laughs" and how she loved them "head to toe." Then she'd turn around and start talking about how annoying some of the boys in her classes were. She was only eight years old when we lived at our grandparents', so we naturally didn't expect much from her.

When it was my turn, I didn't have any reservations in telling the truth. I didn't think much about how my siblings always mentioned the opposite sex, and I always mentioned the boy that I was too scared to talk to in class, because I thought he was the most beautiful creature I had ever laid my eyes on.

I remember it very clearly, how my older brothers would look at me with these weird smiles on their faces and ask me about some of my friends who were girls, and whether I thought they were pretty or not. If I did, I said yes, I think she's really pretty!

But did I have a crush on her? Nah. That's gross, she's just my friend.

This continued for the whole six months we lived at our grandparents' house.

My sister was probably too young to understand it, but that's how my brothers have known for a long time that I'm gay: because I've been gay since I knew what having a crush on someone was.

Fast forward in time to me at a little older age, when I actually did have a blazing hot fire crush on someone. He was a boy. The fact that he was a boy, when all my friends were having crushes on girls, brought on the self-consciousness I mentioned earlier. I didn't feel that my crush on a boy was wrong, but I did feel like I was being left out of something.

Obviously I didn't hide my shyness well, because as soon as I got home from school the day I realized what was happening, my brothers pulled me into my bedroom and asked me what was the matter. Out of earshot of my parents, of course.

My sister invaded the room with her loud off-key singing and was immediately silenced by Isaac. The room became this dark, serious environment with my three siblings crowded around me, concerned about why their little brother Grant looked so gloomy.

I told them I realized something, and I was unsure about it and that nobody knew.

At the same time, all three of them asked what it was, and I stayed quiet. I felt very crowded and couldn't speak. Jake somehow understood—older brother's intuition, maybe?—and pushed Isaac and Carol out of the room gently.

He sat next to me, and I revealed that I had developed a crush on this boy called Adam Tovel, and I didn't know what to do about it.

"We've known you like boys since a long time ago," said Jake, "at Grandma's and Grandpa's. What's the problem with liking Adam?"

"Because he's a boy," I said.

"So, what's the problem?"

"All my friends like girls, and my girl friends like boys. None of the boys like boys and none of the girls like girls."

"Maybe they're just not telling you," he said.

I hadn't thought about it like that before.

"I'm not sure I want to like a boy," I said.

"Why not?"

These were really hard questions for me to answer, but I'm glad Jake asked them to me, because it did help save a lot of grief in the future to understand my sexuality earlier than a lot of people.

He asked me if I didn't want to like a boy because it made me feel like I stood out in a way that didn't feel too comfortable. When he asked that, it made sense, and I said yes.

"Well," he said, and I can still see him sitting back on the floor with his arms crossed like he does when he's serious about something. "If you ask me, there's nothing wrong with you liking a boy. We're all human, anyway."

Man, my brother was wise back then. Not that he isn't now, but when you're younger, things impact you more strongly.

I felt pretty good about the whole thing, not that I was going to go blabbing to the whole class that I liked Adam Tovel and wanted him to be my first kiss, but I wasn't as worried as I'd been a few minutes before.

I didn't tell my parents that night, or even attempt a discussion until a few years later. Which, speaking real time, wasn't too long ago from right now.

It's not because I'm not close with my parents. I guess I'm as close to them as any eighteen-year-old guy can be, especially one who's highly involved in his sports life/career, and trying to survive school, and maintain a social life.

However, the topic of my sexuality isn't a discussion I particularly wanted to bring up with them until the unavoidable time came, and I hoped that wouldn't be for a while. It wasn't that I wanted to hide anything from them. I just wasn't ready to come out yet. I wanted to wait until I knew I was ready.

We'll talk more about that later.

Not only did I avoid talking about it with my parents for a long time, but also with my friends. Even though Jake affirmed me from day one, I still felt a little out of place with my teammates, especially the older we got, because they grew more and more outspoken about their girlfriends (and what they were doing together) and more involved in who's-dating-who.

Seeing many of them dating, I felt like I was missing out on something, and I wanted to find out what that something was. So, I decided that I'd get into a relationship with a girl to try it out. I knew I liked guys, but maybe I just didn't know that I liked girls yet. You never know until you try, right?

Either way, if I started dating a girl, it would make me look like I was keeping up with the rest of the guys. And I definitely wanted to keep up with the rest of the guys.

Normally I would have talked to Jake about my plan to start dating girls, but this time I didn't. It was something I wanted to think about to myself first, and ask him what he thought afterwards.

So I started thinking as hard as I could about it, which isn't something I usually do. I don't like to over think anything. I like to live by my gut, which often gets me into trouble, but I'm learning to do less stupid stuff as I get older.

Getting into a cycle of playing with my love life was probably a pretty dumb decision, though. But it was one that helped me be who I am today, and this is what I want to share with you.

By the way, Adam Tovel was not my first kiss.

Chapter 2

One of the first things I thought about really hard was which girl seemed the most datable at the time.

Beginning to date someone took some planning. I couldn't just walk up to a random girl and be like, "You want to date me? Let's date." Like how you go into a gas station and buy a bottle of water. People don't work that way.

So, I went through the people I follow on Instagram and looked at all the girls' profiles. A lot of people in high school put their relationship status in their bio, so it wasn't too hard to tell who was single and who was taken. Not to mention, the girls who were already dating someone typically had lots of photos of them and their boyfriends up.

It took hours of my time, and I got frustrated with not being able to pick a girl, so I took a break.

I thought I could start thinking about how to let them know I was interested.

But my mind stayed pretty blank for a long time. *This is a lot harder than I expected,* I thought. I know better now, but back then I wondered if dating was always this hard.

After football practice, we were all in the locker room getting changed and showered. The whole room stunk like something died in there. We were all covered in sweat and grass and some of us were bleeding a little. Someone also had let out a nasty fart, but we'll never know who because no one claimed it.

Sometimes I wonder why I'm so attracted to boys when they can smell so bad, but I think it's because I actually like the rough, raw, smelly, messy habits guys have. Not all, but some. I'm a football player, so that's just what I'm around all the time. Plus, guys who play sports can have super-hot bodies.

But I digress.

My locker was next to a guy called Skarzelli. His name was really Damien, but most of us were called by our last names. Skarzelli was the team captain, and also one of the most social guys at school. He and I were pretty close and hung out a few times a week with the rest of our friends.

Skarz also had a tendency to date a lot of girls within each semester. It was unclear whether he was ever in an actual relationship with any of them, or whether he just had a ton of flings with girls instead of pursuing anything serious.

I'll try to retell it as closely as possible.

"Yo, Skarz," I said while we were getting our change of clothes out of our lockers. "I've got a dilemma."

"What's that?"

"Well," I had to act this out like I really meant it, "I've got my eyes on a couple of girls."

"Yeah?" He grinned. This was his favorite thing to talk about.

"Yeah, but I don't know if they're single."

"Who are they?"

I thought about how I had given up after spending so much time searching on Instagram, so instead of looking awkward while I tried to think of names, I unscrewed my water bottle and took a big gulp. *I should have been expecting this question,* I thought. *Stupid me!*

While I was swallowing, I thought of a genius way to use Skarz's social personality to find out who was single.

"Well, I don't want to say yet," I lied, knowing I had no names in mind, and winked at him. Hopefully it wasn't a flirty wink, because I'll be honest, he did have a good smell to him, and a great six-pack. What can I say, I'm easily attracted.

I continued: "Tell me a couple of girls you know who are single, and I'll tell you if they're the ones I've been looking at."

I hope he names some people I at least vaguely know, I thought.

Skarz pulled his shirt on. I could see he was giving it some thought. He knew practically everyone in the school somehow. I couldn't understand how he kept so many people straight in his head. His memory must have been fantastic.

He unwrapped a protein bar and bit off half of it. "Hmm. Alison is single, she was talking to Warren a couple of months ago but nothing came of it."

"Alison in Physics class, you mean?"

"Yeah, that Alison."

I knew which one he was talking about. She had great hair and nice fashion sense. We had done a group project with a few other people before. But it was one of those that you had to get done within one class, like a pop quiz sort of. So we didn't talk that much.

"Megan was single, but last week she started dating Adam."

"Adam Tovel?" I asked.

"Yeah, him."

Obviously, Adam Tovel was not gay. That's why he wasn't my first kiss. I found that out quickly when I overheard him bragging to a couple of guys in sixth grade about kissing some girl in the bathroom when no one was looking. We never really became friends, but we had most classes together since starting high school.

If we're being totally honest, and I mean totally because I'm confessing here, Wentworth Miller (the guy from the TV show Prison Break) was my first kiss, but it's just because I came home drunk late one night after going crazy with some of my teammates, and he popped in my head. I looked him up on my phone in bed, and kissed the screen right where his mouth was because he was just so good looking to drunk me. And he's actually gay, in real life, so I thought, at least while

I was drunk, that maybe there would be a chance one day, even though that's impossible because he's famous and I'm not. I'll probably never act in Hollywood. Unless they need real football players for a movie.

"Talia just broke up a couple of days ago with her boyfriend. Pretty rough breakup, too."

Yes! I knew Talia. We weren't great friends, which was even better for this situation, but we knew the same people. She had dark, exotic eyes and walked in a way that turned the heads of every guy in school.

I may be gay, but I know a gorgeous girl when I see one.

"What happened there?" I asked.

Skarz drank his bottle of water in one gulp. "Apparently he was talking to a girl from another school, and that girl tagged him in a party photo on Instagram. Talia didn't know the girl and wasn't invited to that party, so she flipped."

"How do you know?"

"I've known Talia for a while, so she talks to me sometimes." He winked. "Anyone who scores her is a lucky guy indeed, let me just say that much."

I laughed in a way I hope didn't sound too nervous. Obviously I had no idea what I was getting myself into, and now Skarzelli knew I was up for the taking. There was no backing out.

This, though, was a great opportunity. Talia had just broken up with her boyfriend. He was on the verge of cheating, if he hadn't already.

She needed a rebound while it was still fresh.

I was willing to be that rebound.

"So?" Skarz asked.

"So what?"

"Any of these girls your chosen few?"

I nodded. "Yeah. All three of them, actually."

It wasn't true, as you already know. But I was determined to find out if dating girls was my thing, after all.

Later at home when I was alone in my room, I couldn't help thinking how my teammates made it seem like dating their girlfriends was the best think in the world. *Maybe I'll learn to like that too.*

We both know it was a lie, but it sounded reasonable enough to me at that time. Besides, I wasn't ready to date a guy. Didn't even know where to find one.

I picked a photo from Talia's feed and sent her a message about how pretty it was.

From there, we started talking a little. She always answered my messages within 10 minutes, and our conversations got longer and longer until we were both walking into school every morning like zombies, but smiled secretly at each other when we passed in the hallway.

So I did what I thought any guy should do. After school, I met her at her locker. All her friends were there, which was great because they could all smell my cologne and see me put my arm up on the lockers. I talked to all of them like I'd known them for a long time.

Next thing I knew, Talia and I were eating lunch together, going out of our way to just say hey, and arranging for study sessions on the weekends.

Word quickly got around that we two were becoming a thing.

Maybe dating's not as hard as I thought.

The first study session started with us in an old library in Boston city. She didn't live too far from me, maybe about 15 minutes, so I picked her up, and we lugged all our books into that old dusty building. We whispered to each other while we walked through each floor, trying to find a secluded spot to spread out and not get any work done.

I surprised myself with how quickly I evolved into this guy who seemingly knew just what to do to get a girl, and how to respond to her moves. Maybe I had just been subconsciously soaking in what my friends had done for years, or watched too many movies.

Either way, I looked like I knew exactly what I was doing, and I was proud of myself. I still didn't really feel sexually or romantically attracted to her, but I knew she was gorgeous and she seemed to like me.

Of course we didn't get much studying done at the library. You know how those things usually work out. It ends up with some serious sexual tension, which was tough for me because I still didn't feel it towards Talia, but I let her go with whatever it took.

Maybe, just maybe, I would warm up to being with a girl. Maybe if I took it a little further.

We left, and I drove her home, but she told me to go another way. I didn't know the small road she asked me to turn on, but I did it, and it led down a path through a lot of trees and eventually came to a dead end.

I'll let you imagine what happened next. I don't want to go into too many details.

When it was all said and done, I honestly didn't feel too different. I wish I could say I did, but my brain was still trying to convince myself.

Maybe just take it a little further. Maybe just keep going with it. A lot of people take a long time to warm up to this.

I should have known then and there that this wasn't going to go according to plan. I knew I was gay, through and through.

What was the fascination with girls? Maybe, if I kept trying, I'd understand.

I tried to trick my mind into thinking that would happen, but I knew it wouldn't.

Talia and I kept going with whatever it was we had going on. I liked her as a person but had no emotional connection whatsoever. We lasted for several weeks and never officially put a label on anything. I never did have that burning feeling towards her that my friends had towards the girls they dated, but I always morphed into someone very different when I was with her. She seemed to like it, and there was some kind of thrill I got when I became that different person.

One day she came to me and said she wanted to see other guys; not that I wasn't special, but she didn't want to hurt me.

I wasn't heartbroken, of course. I said that's fine, and I thanked her for communicating with me. We never spoke to each other again. Not in a hostile way, but neither of us cared to remain friends with our exes.

It was fine with me.

I had dated Talia, I was one of the top players on the football team, and I was going to college on a football scholarship. I was officially a hot shot at school. Girls started hanging around me like they did with the other guys, and I felt more "in" with the guys.

I became a master in the art of the tease. It became part of my façade when I was with friends from school, and it was fun to act like someone else.

But I wasn't getting what I'd hoped to out of it.

For a few months I fooled around with a few different girls, nothing serious, but never went "all the way" with them. I killed them with the tease. I'd give them just enough to make them crazy for more, then call it a night. My friends wouldn't have been able to keep this up, but the reason I could is because the more girls that came to me, and the more I messed around with them, the less my body responded to any of it. I just kept doing it, well, for the heck of it I guess. It's hard to consciously break a reputation.

I found myself going home at night, sometimes drunk, wishing I had a boyfriend to sleep with. Some warm (male) body to be there with me.

These feelings were worse when I'd been drinking.

I wasn't ready to come out yet, but I knew I was getting closer to that point.

Only once in all that time of playing my "alter ego" did I almost come out. I was seeing Megan, one of the girls Skarzelli had mentioned in the locker room that day. She was great. Like with Talia, I was a rebound. She had just broken up with Adam Tovel, and her way to deal with stress (like mine) was to go crazy at parties. We both had fake IDs. Most people I knew did. They're pretty common nowadays, anyway, and I already look a lot older than I am, so mine can slide even at public bars.

But at house parties we didn't need the fake IDs. Rich kids invited a bunch of people when their parents were gone on business trips and such, and kept it on the down-low, so only certain people knew when and where to go.

Megan and I were driving separately since I had practice until later in the evening. I got cleaned up in the locker room, put on my game face, and left for the party. My parents thought I was heading out to eat and to see a movie with some teammates, who were also going to the party.

We got there and immediately started having a great time. I put on my "mask" and played exclusive to Megan the whole night. We danced, drank, laughed, had a good time.

At one point we were standing by the wall, both of us pretty intoxicated, and she asked me to tell her a secret. I didn't think twice about it, especially since I knew she was also out of her mind a little.

"I used to have a crush on your ex," I yelled over the music in her ear, and we both laughed.

"My ex?" she yelled back, still laughing.

"Adam Tovel, right?"

She tripped over her feet and a little beer spilled on the floor. We both laughed again. "Yeah, I dated Adam! You had a crush on…Adam?"

"Yeah!"

"You had a crush on him? You know he's a guy, right?"

I didn't understand at first, and then I realized what I had said. I laughed it off and took another sip of beer.

"I didn't have a crush on Adam," I corrected myself. "I used to have class with him."

"Oh!" She put her hand on my neck. "I thought you said you had a crush on him!"

I knew it would be okay. We would blame it on the alcohol, if we remembered at all. Being in character, I leaned over and kissed Megan, like I was trying to make myself feel better for the screw up I almost made.

She never mentioned that incident, and I never brought it up either.

It didn't matter either way, because the truth would be out sooner than I expected.

Chapter 3

"I need to get out for a while," I said.

We had Monday off school, and for the long weekend, I didn't want to be around anyone I knew. I needed to get away and be myself. Forget about life for a couple of days.

I wanted to find a guy. Any guy. I'll admit it: I was desperate.

Even though I kept trying to find some comfort and good sensation in being with girls, I always felt left high and dry. And I knew that, through dating these girls, I was getting closer to coming out.

Since I was about to be in college anyway, I wanted to get an early start with the social life part of it. I wanted to see if people in college were really as open-minded and fun as all high school students glorified them to be.

And since Boston is a big city, I knew that the chances of seeing any of my classmates or teammates at a bar were unlikely. Namely, a gay bar.

I was one of the few lucky ones that looked a lot older than my actual age. My fake ID says I'm 22, which I could easily pass for. I could have made it older but I didn't want to stretch it.

Skarz said I could use him as an excuse to get out for a night, and I took him up on that offer. He didn't know what I was going to do, and he didn't need to.

A few of my teammates and I were used to saying, "Yeah, just say you're with me" to get each other out of a bind. It wasn't the most honest thing, but it worked. The majority of the time, the getaway probably had something to do with girls.

I didn't tell them otherwise, this time. Only that I needed to go.

So when I told my parents that I needed to spend the weekend away, I namedropped him and they barely thought about it again.

"That's fine, honey. Have fun." The typical parent phrase.

Oh, boy, was I going to have fun.

I knew exactly what I was going to do. Depending how it ended, I might actually be gone the whole weekend, or just later that night (early morning, rather).

I had only done this once before, almost a year ago. This time I knew I had a better chance because I'd grown an inch since last time. When I went out by myself last time, I didn't have a problem getting into any of the bars or clubs except one. The bouncer had taken one look at me and knew I was using a fake ID. The rest didn't care.

That was an awesome night, but I was with a couple of teammates so I had to tone it down a little. I talked to one guy that night, but made sure not to do anything the guys would find suspicious.

But tonight, I was going out by myself to be whoever I felt like being.

Truthfully, I was pretty tired of keeping up the façade at school. It brought me some adrenaline at first, but by now it was driving me into a place of loneliness instead of companionship. I hate to think about things too much, but it was making me more angry than anything.

All the time lately I had been thinking about when I had my crush on Adam Tovel and Jake told me it was okay.

Did I have a problem with liking guys? No. Not at all.

Really, I don't even care what other people think. I'm not going to do something if I'm not ready, and that's the only reason I hadn't officially come out (like I said earlier). I just didn't know if I was missing any opportunities to enjoy life like how my friends were doing, getting girlfriends and going through the usual routine of all that. As we can tell, my efforts and current reputation were having the reverse effect on me. And my whole idea that the more time I spent with girls and the more I did with them, the more I'd like them…didn't work at all.

I get that some people don't need to try. To each his own.

But do I regret any of it? Nah. In fact, I'm proud of myself for venturing out and doing something different, something that made me a little uncomfortable.

I was getting close to graduation, and the reality was sinking in that I was about to be independent, going to college on a scholarship, meeting new people. It all seemed too good to be true, and I couldn't wait.

So, when my parents said the "Have fun, honey" line, I felt my blood pump through my body like I had just run the length of the field while carrying a hundred-pound weight.

I didn't really need to bring anything with me, maybe an extra shirt that I'd keep in my car. Worst case, I could just get a shirt from a store or somewhere. I wasn't going too far, just into the city, but it was perfectly far enough for me to let loose.

No one knew me where I was going, anyway. It would be fine.

I was packing and Jake barged into my room, asking a ton of questions about what I was going to be doing over the weekend. I didn't want to tell him, not because I wanted to hide, but I just wanted to be alone. I tried to be really vague but he kept pushing me to answer.

Jake had quickly found out about me dating a lot of girls after I came home late one night, and I couldn't help but tell him what had just happened. It was that evening with Talia, when she told me to go on the little side road. It was my first key experience with a girl, and it wasn't all it was cracked up to be, based on what the other guys always said.

Jake had told me it was okay, but not to push myself. Which of course made me want to push myself and keep going. I was sure that if I gave it enough time, I'd warm up and fall in love with a girl. The guys were just having such a great time with their girlfriends and I wanted to have a relationship like that.

I just needed time away for myself. That's what I told Jake, that I needed to go decompress for a while. I had the weekend off from football practice, and we were supposed to do a lot of exercise in our free time, which of course only a few of the guys would actually do.

I'd heard there were some parties going on and apparently a lot of people were getting ready to enjoy the weekend to the fullest. A lot of people asked me if I was going, almost like they were expecting me to go, but I told them I had some other stuff to do.

I told myself to hurry up and get dressed and leave so Jake couldn't talk to me for much longer. Luckily he quit asking so many questions, but he was too good at putting the puzzle pieces together.

"You going to see a guy?"

"I don't have a guy to see," I told him. "I'm just going to blow off some steam."

He did that arm-crossing thing again. "Be careful, all right?"

"Yeah, yeah." Of course I was going to be careful.

"You're my little brother, I gotta make sure you're okay."

He was starting to make me angry, so I told him to quit wasting his energy and focus on his own life. I was in control of mine.

I know I shouldn't have said it like that. I do that all the time, get upset at people for caring about me. Mostly my family, because Skarz and the other guys were too obsessed with their own lives.

Kind of like I was.

Jake knew I was beginning to boil, so he left, which made me even angrier, so I decided it would be best for me to leave. I went out the door almost without saying bye to anyone, got in the car, and drove into the city.

What I did last time was park in a church that never had cars in the parking lot. There was a bus stop right in front of the church that led straight into the city, and that was how I got around. I didn't want to drive drunk. I wasn't that stupid (no one should be that stupid). One of my teammate's brother died because he was driving drunk, not even going that fast, but ran off the road in just the right place to total the car and him.

We all learned from that, because we had all driven home drunk one time or another. None of us did it again.

It was barely sundown, so I sat in my car and listened to music and wasted time on my phone until it was time to go.

Weeks before, I would have spent that time looking at photos of girls to try to rouse something up in me. This time, I looked at pictures of guys.

I got a little nervous, because I actually was alone tonight. I made a pact with myself that if I went into a place and saw anyone who looked remotely familiar, I would leave and go to another bar.

The bus took me downtown, where I got off and chilled in a fast food joint for a while until it got late enough to go scout for a club. I wished I had had a drink to loosen me up, but I was going into this sober.

I was crazy excited.

I decided to start at a couple of "regular" bars, and, when I felt ready, I'd move on to some designated gay spots in the area. That's exactly what I did: got a little tipsy, danced with a couple of girls who were already wasted, but didn't spend more time with them than I needed to and definitely didn't hit on them.

In the first gay bar, I didn't know quite what to do at first, so I ordered a drink and stood by the wall half-hidden in a shadow.

Some guy came up and struck up a conversation. This is where time started to blur for me. The drinks were beginning to take their toll, and I didn't mind at all. All I could do was look at this guy's face and smile. He yelled something at the bartender like they were friends, and in a second handed me a shot.

I heard him say "Cheers" into my ear, and we took the shots.

Later I saw his face in the light. He didn't look too much older than me, which was cool. He had a great smile.

To be honest I don't remember much about that club. I do recall looking around every now and then for people I might know, but when I thought about it, I didn't know anyone from school who would be at a gay bar by themselves. They were all at one of the house parties going on, anyway.

The guy pulled me aside at one point in the night to rest after we danced so hard we were both sweating. All I remember is he asked my name, and I told him Grant, and he told me his name was Micah.

He kissed me then. It was way better than kissing Wentworth Miller on my phone screen.

I swear I can't remember any concrete details about what happened next except my heart beating really hard from excitement. This was turning into everything I had been wanting so bad.

Why did I try to be something else for so long when I've been cool with being gay the whole time? I wondered at some point in my hazy memory.

Anything else about that night comes back to my head in little flashes that aren't clear, so I'm not sure if it's my head making any of it up or if it's true.

I remember walking down the road with him, our arms together. And then laughing in the back of a car. Going up some stairs and into a room.

We didn't turn the lights on.

My memory resumes in the morning, which actually was noon. I woke up slowly and had an awful hangover. Beside me was the guy, who cleared his throat and said, "Hi, Grant."

I said, "Good morning, Micah." How I managed to remember his name is beyond me.

We lay there beside each other in the dark room. Only a little sunlight came in through the curtains, but even that little streak of it made my eyeballs hurt like hell.

I felt like I couldn't move. Micah handed me a bottle of water and I drank the whole thing without thinking twice.

"Are you hungry?"

I was starving. The last time I had eaten was before my night started, and that was just a cheap burger and some floppy fries. The grease clearly hadn't done much to help lessen a hangover.

Then again, I had no idea how much I had drunk.

Even though I was hung over big time, I was happier than I had ever been. It felt so natural to be with a guy, even if just for a short time.

This must be how the other guys felt when they were with a girl.

I had definitely been missing out, but not how I thought before.

Micah told me he had no food that was good for breakfast, so we'd better go out and get something decent.

This was my first time really being with a guy, and I was a little awkward. I guess he could tell, because he was nice and made me feel comfortable by touching my shoulder when he walked past me. He even gave me a few kisses, and I thought my heart was going to beat out of my chest.

We walked down the street toward a diner he said was the usual hangover spot. The sun would have blinded me if he hadn't let me borrow a spare pair of sunglasses. In the better light, I looked him up and down as we walked. I felt pretty lucky.

He took my hand as we walked down the road, and my first instinct was to jerk my hand away in case anyone I knew was around. But we were in a part of town I had never really been in before, so I decided to take a risk and hold his hand back.

We got a couple of glances, but I was too tired to notice them much. I didn't notice much of anything the rest of the day, actually. It was just a chill day, eating our meal slowly and walking around until we could barely stand anymore.

Micah asked me all about myself, and I told him everything he wanted to know. I learned some about him, too: he was from the Boston area, a sophomore in college, studying architecture, and was openly gay.

When he was younger, his mom had left his dad for another woman, but it wasn't an ugly divorce. His dad, surprisingly, was supportive of his mom. So when he came out, his family was understanding.

I told him that's pretty different than my situation. Not that my parents weren't understanding, but I'd never talked with them about it before. My siblings were supportive, especially my older brother. No one else knew yet.

He asked why not.

I snapped at him, like I did my brother. I didn't want him to pry, because I didn't like to think about it too much. I wanted to handle this little by little, taking action with my gut instead of brooding over it in my head for hours and hours.

He seemed pretty shocked that I got upset so quickly. We barely knew each other, and after such a good day and night together, I didn't want to ruin anything. So I apologized, and I even kissed him to make sure he knew I was sorry.

It was okay after that. We talked about having no plans for the long weekend, originally wanting to spend it alone until we found each other. He had gotten a text earlier from some friends wanting him to come out, but he said no, he had something else come up, and looked at me with a smile.

We walked slowly back to his place and spent the rest of the night there.

I felt incredible.

The next morning we woke up feeling hangover-free and happy to see each other.

My first thought was that I needed to go home that day or my parents would start wondering where I was.

In the back of my head I wondered about what dating a guy would be like, and whether I would ever see Micah again or would today be the last time.

I wasn't sure which of those I preferred. Only having a good time with him for a weekend seemed mysterious and special, and it seemed like seeing him again or starting something with him would kind of ruin that.

He and I didn't talk about it. By the looks of it, he didn't have anything major on his mind. We didn't leave his apartment that afternoon except to go downstairs and get the food we ordered in.

That afternoon was like any afternoon a couple would spend together, away from everyone else. Just having quality time, not worried about the world outside the windows or what would happen the next day.

At last I checked my phone and saw that it was past dinnertime. I told Micah I had to leave.

"So soon?" he asked.

Yeah, I told him. My family will be worried, and I needed to get ready for school Monday.

I guess he thought I looked pretty blue about it, because he came close to me and made me forget the world for the next hour.

After what was probably the best experience of my life, I got dressed and quietly left, making sure I had everything I brought, which was only my wallet and phone. The extra shirt was back in my car. I would definitely need it before I got home because this shirt still smelled like alcohol.

I had a lot of time to myself on the way back to my car, and I didn't think about anything except reflecting on the incredible time I had with Micah. I felt like a new person, like I finally had gotten in touch with myself and knew what I wanted and what I liked. I was pretty proud of myself, too, for going out alone, doing what I wanted, and not going too crazy.

The bus took forever to arrive, moved slowly in the long weekend's evening traffic, and finally pulled up to my stop at the quiet neighborhood near the church.

There was only one streetlight in the area. I saw some birds fly into the trees and heard crickets. My car was still parked in the church's parking lot, thank goodness. In my opinion, it would take a pretty heartless person to steal a car from a church's parking lot. The only people I'd seen in that area were old, anyway, and old people like to live in safe areas. That's one reason why I chose this church.

Nothing like cranking up the car and blaring some music while driving real fast home. Driving sober and happy and feeling refreshed.

I thought nothing could bring me down now.

Man, I was ready to finish off my last year of high school as the chick magnet and then leave all that behind when I graduated.

I felt like I ruled the world.

Chapter 4

I didn't think anything was different that night or the next day when my phone barely dinged off.

Usually I at least get a few notifications from social media and a few texts every day, but there was nothing. Honestly I was kind of glad, because I wasn't ready to return to "real life" yet. I wanted to relish in the secret couple of days I had.

I got home when my parents were already asleep, which was better for me because I didn't feel like talking.

Of course, when I don't feel like talking is when my brothers come in, and my sister's ears perk up to the three of us talking and she pops up, too.

It started with Jake coming in, curious about my last couple of days with no contact, and when Isaac heard us talking about something that sounded secret or scandalous, he poked his head into the room and asked what happened.

Jake told him that I was with a guy over the weekend.

I told Jake I never said that. (Sneaky of me, but true.)

He asked where I was; I said with a friend.

"Which friend?"

"Not one that either of you know."

Carol came in and plopped down on my bed, spilling a few drops of tea on my blanket. She was obsessed with everything British at the time (still is) and drank at least two or three cups of tea every day.

I tried to push her off the bed so she wouldn't spill any more, but she wouldn't budge, so I gave her an evil look and gave up.

"What's his name?" she asked.

I told them I had never said I was with a guy over the weekend.

They kept trying to make arguments to get the truth out of me.

Demands like: then who were you with? Because you're not old enough to get a hotel room by yourself, and there's no reason for you to get a hotel room unless you're with somebody.

"Not necessarily. People get hotel rooms to write books and make art in solitude all the time." I thought I was clever.

Carol asked if that's what I was doing for the past two days, and Isaac started laughing his head off.

I said I wasn't writing a book or making art, and I didn't have a hotel room with anybody.

Wishing they would let it go, I sat there looking at my phone, pretending to do other things for a few minutes while they tried to pry the weekend out of me, but it didn't work.

"Come on," Jake told me. "We're not gonna tell anyone. Mom and Dad will never find out."

"What makes you think I was doing something I want to hide from them?" I asked.

Isaac had been staring at me for a while, and I saw a glimmer in his eyes.

He figured it out.

"You slept with a guy," he said proudly.

I felt my heart beat behind my eyeballs and I said no, that's not what happened, but Carol was already looking at me in the same knowing way, and Jake's jaw was dragging on the floor now, and I got so flustered I couldn't defend myself well enough.

"You slept with a guy!" Jake repeated, and a huge smile came across his face. He pounced on me and starting rubbing my head with his knuckles, saying a lot of ridiculous things to me while Isaac and Carol laughed.

I told them to shut up or we would wake up Mom and Dad.

"So did you?" Carol asked.

"No," I said, but of course they knew it was a lie.

"How was it?"

I wasn't going to give them any of the information they wanted.

Isaac asked some really immature stuff that made me wish I could disappear: how big was he? How big am I? Was I the top or bottom? Do guys spoon like hetero couples do? I couldn't bring myself to answer any of it.

The whole time Jake just watched what was happening with his stupid older brother expression on his face.

I started to get ticked off and told them to leave me alone, that what happened this weekend was private to me, and no one else needed to know about it. And I got serious about it, because I wasn't in the mood for them to spoil anything.

They know I get angry easily, so they backed off and started joking to each other.

Growing up with two older brothers and a younger sister, I've gotten used to them making fun of everything. I join in sometimes, too, but you could say I'm moodier than they are. We all gang up on each other sometimes, of course. All in good fun.

The best way to get them to stop was just to keep ignoring them, so I distracted myself on my phone, and when that got boring, I started to clean my room. It was my strategy, just a little. If Mom had any questions about where I had been, she would forget because she'd be so glad I finally cleaned up. Football gear and general teenage-boy-athlete is a hard smell to get rid of.

Or so I hear, because I can't smell it unless it's in the locker room.

Anyway.

Around midnight they finally stopped talking, and we all said goodnight. When they were gone, the silence was so nice.

I turned out the lights and thought about how I had woken up several times in the past couple of days with someone else next to me.

Whatever came of Micah and me, he definitely helped me learn a lot about myself.

I wasn't sure how I felt about seeing him again. Should I or shouldn't I? Before I left, he had put his number in my phone, but I hadn't decided yet whether to text him or not. I don't stay friends with my exes; was he was an ex in some sort of way, or potentially more than that?

I knew something in me wanted more, but not immediately. I had already established myself as a certain type of guy at school, and coming out publicly wasn't something I wanted to do just yet. Sometime soon, but not yet.

Here was my ideal: I wanted to take it slow and only tell people when I felt like it. But most importantly I just didn't want to spend so much energy defending myself or explaining when or where or why I wanted to come out.

Isn't that simple enough?

I was almost asleep, still caught up in my happy thoughts, when I heard my door move. It was Jake.

Sitting up, I asked him what he was doing and did he need something.

He said Isaac and Carol were asleep, and he wanted to talk to his little brother alone, just to make sure everything was fine.

"I know we made you upset earlier, and I want to know if anything bad happened this weekend."

The fact that he wasn't harassing me and was treating me like an adult made me a lot more comfortable. I relaxed and told him no, actually the opposite happened. The weekend was amazing.

"How so?"

Without saying too much, I told him I was blowing off some tension I'd accumulated during the semester so far, especially from dating so many girls, and having the pressure on me to perform well in football to make sure I kept my scholarship.

Jake already knew I had a fake ID, so he wasn't surprised that I went out drinking by myself. Isaac had a fake one, too, but he didn't have the guts to go out in public yet, and partying wasn't really his scene anyway.

"So this guy was something special, huh?"

I said yeah.

"Did you know him before?"

I said nah.

"You stayed with him the whole time?"

"Yeah."

Jake seemed okay with it, and the most teasing he gave me was a wink and a slap on my shoulder. He said all right, and that he just wanted to check on me.

I have a good brother. Well, he's good sometimes.

"You gonna keep dating girls?"

"I don't think so." I knew that was the better decision. Every day graduation was getting closer and closer, and if I wanted to keep the scholarship I'd already gotten, I needed to focus hard. Also, I couldn't bear to keep doing what I'd been doing with girls. It was okay while it lasted, but after the weekend with Micah, I knew it would be impossible from now on.

"Okay," said Jake, and he left the room with a goodnight. I turned the light back out and went to sleep, mentally getting ready for practice the next day.

It was so nice not waking up at 5:00 a.m. for practice before school. Long weekends are the best.

I woke up around 10:00 and had a slow day, not really doing anything. I hung around the house and was lazy until it was time to go to practice in the late afternoon.

The weather was good, and the wind was blowing just the right amount. I'm not one to remember details like that, but I remember every detail this time because that day changed everything for me.

I felt so good, driving fast with my windows down, feeling great after my special weekend and ready to brave the next semester before heading off to start my real life and career at college. With a scholarship, too! It's like college was basically paying me to play football.

How much greater could life get?

I was always one of the first to get to practice, and I changed with a couple of the other guys and headed out to the field. I liked to get started early, even if I wasn't really doing anything, because it showed the coach that I was responsible and would be great doing this full-time later on.

One by one the rest of the guys arrived and joined us out there, and practice officially started. We worked our butts off, and I didn't even want to complain once.

This mattered more to me now. I had fresh enthusiasm.

Sure, I had tried being with girls, and it wasn't bad, but it definitely wasn't my thing. I'm glad I tried it, because otherwise I would have been asking "what if" at some point, probably.

I had never had an experience with a guy like that, and now I felt like a new person. I was excited to finally get to know myself in a different way, and I was more confident about anything I'd ever questioned in regard to myself.

If I was ready to graduate and get on with life before, now I was more than ever. I could have graduated that night after practice and started college the next day and been happy.

After practice, something else happened.

Let me just say, sometimes life doesn't happen the way you plan it. Sometimes things happen that you aren't expecting, and sometimes these things seem like they're going to ruin your life at first.

That's not true at all.

If you leave this story with anything, remember this: you're made to overcome anything. Even if you think life is the worst and you hate everything about every day, don't give up. Figure out what your goal is, and do whatever it takes to get there.

And listen, if people give you a hard time about being gay, don't listen to them. Because it's your life, and you do what you feel is right for you because this is your only one.

Now, for what happened after football practice that day.

We were all covered in sweat and grass and dirt, like usual. We'd practiced for three hours and were exhausted. Some of the guys were complaining to themselves, but not me. I was tired, yeah, but I was still feeling great mentally.

A couple of the guys had to leave immediately and just changed pants and ran out of the locker room. Most of us stayed to shower and freshen up before heading home.

I was opening my locker to get out a plastic bag. I always put my gear in a plastic bag to take home for washing, that way it doesn't get the car so dirty on the way.

As I was stuffing my pants and socks into the bag, I was talking with Skarz about the parties over the weekend. He was acting different, I couldn't tell how, but he wasn't chatting like he normally did with me after practice.

Maybe he had a rough day, I thought.

He continued to act in this weird way until everyone was almost done changing and showering. All the guys were at their lockers now, putting stuff up and tying their shoes.

Skarz cleared his throat and said loudly, "Well, I learned something very unusual this weekend."

This must be why he's acting weird, I thought. One of the guys asked what he learned.

"Let me find it," Skarz said. He got out his phone and looked through it. I didn't think it was anything too important, so I just put my shirt on and went to the mirror to comb my hair.

"I had a great weekend," he finally said, holding his phone up in front of his face. I looked over at him to see he was reading from some text messages.

I figured what he was going to tell us would be of no interest to me, until he read the next message.

"I met this awesome guy. He goes to your school."

I stopped combing my hair, listening for what was next.

"I said, 'Oh really? Who was it?'" Skarz started laughing. "Guys, listen to this. This is what he said, this is what my friend said: 'His name is Grant. He's on the football team.'"

I swear, at this moment my heart actually stopped beating for a full minute, and no doctor can tell me that's not possible because I remember it clearly.

"Do I know Grant? Of course I know Grant!" Skarz started laughing again, and all the guys looked a little confused. Everyone was looking at me at this point.

"What?" I asked, like I didn't know anything.

"So Grant, you met my friend Micah this weekend, right?"

I didn't say anything.

"You know, I've been friends with Micah for several years. We met at the private school I used to go to before transferring here. He's a funny guy." Skarz scrolled through some messages. "You probably noticed he's is unashamedly gay? He'll shout it to the world if the chance comes up."

A few of the guys were starting to put the pieces of this story together; I could see it on their faces. My heart went from not beating to pounding out of my ribcage. I started to get really dizzy.

"Micah told me he met you at the gay bar, Grant. Does this mean you've been pretending to be straight? Or do you have another explanation?"

Some guys let out a loud "Ooooooooh!" and cackled like witches.

"Are you gay, Grant?" One of them asked.

"You don't look gay!" said another one.

"Boys, settle down," said Skarz in his loud football captain voice. "Let's hear it from the horse's mouth, shall we?"

He motioned at me, and I knew I had to say something. They definitely wouldn't understand about why I started dating girls, just to try it out.

I knew I was caught, and now Skarz was being a total dick and outing me in front of the football team, even though he obviously didn't have an issue with Micah being gay since he seemed close to him.

Were all these guys shallow and only cared about football? I had based my friendships with them on nothing but sports and girls, and it seemed they weren't thinking about how I felt right now. They just thought the situation was funny.

I couldn't think of a lie to tell fast enough that would save me from this situation.

Let's pause here, and let me explain something. I wasn't ashamed to be gay. I don't have a problem with it and, quite frankly, I don't think anyone else should either.

What was the most humiliating to me about this situation is the fact that someone was being so horrible and sharing information with a group of people without asking me first. And what's more, if he had a problem with gay people, he wouldn't have been friends with Micah for as long as he said he'd been. He was being completely two-faced in this instance or then he just didn't get it how much this meant to me.

It's normal for people to share pleasurable experiences with people they're close to, so I wasn't angry about Micah telling his friend about a great weekend. However, Skarz was in a position where he should have known he could easily embarrass me, especially with information that's so personal, and he had every option to keep his mouth shut and let me come out when I wanted to.

But instead, he outed me in a really mortifying way, and put me under so much pressure to give an explanation in front of the whole team (except the couple of guys who'd left earlier).

The locker room was quiet, and time slowed down, I'm sure of it. I couldn't see anything clearly because my eyes were blurry. I heard one of the guys snort to hold back a laugh, and I remember hearing words come out of my mouth that I hadn't planned to say.

"Yeah, I'm gay," I said.

The whole locker room erupted into laughter. Actually erupted, like a volcano. I could feel the lava made of laughs surround me.

"You're joking, right?"

"Skarzelli, this is stupid!"

"You want to see the messages?" he asked, and passed around his phone.

The one thing I'm thankful of is that Micah and I hadn't taken any pictures together, but it didn't matter. The words were enough.

Now the whole team knew.

"So you're really…gay?"

I said, yeah, I am.

Someone asked if I was dating Micah. I said no, I'm not dating anyone. They asked about the girls I'd seen; I told them none of them were serious relationships.

I knew what was about to happen. It was evident that not all of my teammates could keep their mouths shut. School was about to be filled with rumors about the gay running back.

Somehow, I stayed calm. It wasn't how I wanted to come out, but what could I do now? Gay or not, I was the one out of the whole team going to college on a scholarship. And not only that, but I had managed to date just as many girls in the last few months as they had managed to date in the last couple of years. The big irony was that I hadn't liked it.

I was too overwhelmed with how suddenly it had happened to lash out and beat Skarz into a pulp on the ground, which is what I would definitely have done otherwise.

What did I do? I didn't say anything else. I finished combing my hair, took my stuff, said bye to everyone except Skarzelli, and walked out while many of them were looking at me, confused.

The last thing I heard was Skarz yelling at them to give his phone back because he didn't want anyone going through his pictures.

On the drive home, I didn't think about anything.

Chapter 5

I walked inside and grabbed a few pieces of pizza. Mom and Dad were yelling over the sound of the vacuum cleaner to Carol, asking her to dust the shelves. Isaac was trying to take out the trash but couldn't tie the bag. Jake was nowhere to be seen.

I just stood there and ate my pizza, still not thinking.

There was nothing to think about. My family was having house cleaning night, and it was chaotic as always. I was about to come out to my parents, and they would probably be a little surprised, and house cleaning night next week would be just the same as it was right now.

Honestly, I wasn't sure if Mom and Dad knew already. They must have heard my siblings talking about it or teasing me, mostly in a good-natured way. Just few weeks before, Isaac said to me "See ya, Gay-rant" on his way out of the door.

I waited until the vacuum was shut off and Dad was winding up the cord. Mom was emptying the dust and dirt out of the inside.

"Hey," I said.

They both said hey and didn't look up.

"I gotta tell you something."

"Okay, honey, that's fine."

"I'm gay."

They both stood up. "Sorry?"

"I'm gay. Just wanted to tell you, if you didn't know already."

Mom looked at me, and I saw the confusion in her face. "You say that so calmly," she said.

I told them it's because I'm sure of who I am, and I don't feel the need to apologize for myself.

Neither of them said anything for a minute. Mom walked over and fixed a glass of ice water for herself. Dad sat down and scratched his ankle.

"I wanted to tell you before you found out anything," I said.

"Anything about what?"

"Well, I was just outed in the locker room."

Jake somehow appeared in the room with us. "You were what?"

"Skarzelli just outed me in the locker room," I said.

Mom asked me if those were football terms, and could I please explain. I told her that "outed" means he exposed the fact that I'm gay. I said he found out, and he told the whole team without my permission, and that rumors were probably going to start flying.

"So I wanted to tell you myself before you might hear it from anyone else."

"Are you okay?" Jake asked.

I told them I was fine, embarrassed at first but fine now.

"You can't let the university know," said Dad.

"Why not?" Jake said.

"That's the first thing you can say?" I couldn't believe it.

Dad told me, "They'll take away your scholarship."

"That stings, Dad. Since when do they take away scholarships for being gay?" I asked.

"But honey," Mom said, "are you sure about this?"

To which I replied, "Definitely."

Dad said, "You don't look gay."

Jake asked him what he thinks gay people look like, and why can't they look like me. I was so grateful that my brother was there.

The honest answer from Dad was that he didn't know gay people could like sports. Jake let out a laugh. "Don't reply to that," he told me.

Dad walked over and said he didn't mean it like that, he really didn't know any better.

"Who I like doesn't affect how I look, Dad," I told him, really trying not to get angry.

This whole time we were talking, Mom was drinking her water and listening. I saw a couple of tears in her eyes, and finally I asked her what was wrong.

"How will you have children?" she cried. "I want you to have children!"

"Mom, I'm only 18," I said.

"There's this thing called 'adoption,' Mom," said Jake.

She nodded, still crying, and wiped her tears with her shirt. She said she was okay now and that she shouldn't be worrying about that right now.

"Just don't let the university know," Dad said again. "You've got to keep your scholarship."

"Why are you so hung up on not letting them know?" I yelled.

"Well, you know the stigma around being gay." Dad almost whispered the word "gay" and proceeded to tell me that he's sure it's happened before.

"That is *not* a good enough reason," I told him, "and I've never heard of anyone losing a scholarship because of who they fall in love with!"

"You need that scholarship. You've worked hard to get it, and not everyone gets it."

Mom started crying again and said she must have messed up somewhere while raising me.

Now I was beginning to get upset. I stood up and quit trying to curb my frustration; I told them that I am not messed up, they didn't make any mistakes, I've known I was gay forever, and it's not because anyone put the idea in my head.

I told them how Jake had been supporting me since I told him about the first boy I had a crush on. Having Jake to listen to my thoughts and help me make decisions like an adult really made accepting myself a lot easier.

"Listen," I said. I was ready for this conversation to be over. Mom had no more tears coming down and was looking all the way down her glass like there was another world in there. Dad and Jake both had their arms crossed and serious expressions on their faces. Carol put her tea in the microwave to warm up.

I can still recall most of what I said because I'm pretty proud of it. I hadn't rehearsed coming out to my family at all. My siblings already knowing made it easier, probably not just for me but also for my parents.

They were all looking at me.

"I don't have it all figured out right now," I told them. "But I'm pretty sure no one does. I know who I am, and I'm confident in that. I don't expect you to understand it right now, or even accept it all the way, but I want to let you know that I'm very happy with who I am."

I reminded my parents that I was mostly talking to them, since Jake and Isaac and Carol already knew.

"Wait, where's Isaac?" Dad asked.

"The trash can probably ate him," said Carol.

"Can you just let me finish talking so I can go rest?" I said.

Mom told me I needed to mop the floor before I rested. I told her, fine, I would do it.

"But seriously," I tried again. "I will eventually learn more about myself than I know right now, but the fact that I'm cool with everything about myself is a big step. Especially at my age, with all these changes that are going to happen soon, college and my football career, all that stuff."

My parents nodded. I thought, *good, they're getting something I'm saying.*

"Now listen, me being gay is only a part of me, and no one should see me differently because of it."

"Just like none of you should be distressed when I move to England one day," said Carol.

Jake told her to be quiet; now wasn't the time for her British BS.

"Jake, be nice," said Mom.

"Yeah, Jake, be nice," Carol echoed.

I thought my family was hopeless, and I rolled my eyes.

Dad noticed that I was losing energy, and he told me that this was a lot to take in suddenly, and he would take a while to warm up to it. Mom agreed. They both said that since I had a lot of those life changes I'd mentioned coming soon, they would still support me.

"...while you figure things out," Dad said, and I knew he meant about the gay part.

"If you're talking about being gay, that's one thing I don't have to figure out. So that makes my life a little easier," I told him.

Carol chuckled and said she was going to get ready for bed and listen to some podcasts, and then she was gone. Before any of us could say anything, Isaac slammed open the door and stripped down to his underwear. He was totally covered in mud. I'm pretty sure all of us forgot that I'd just come out, because we were trying to figure how he'd gotten so dirty. Isaac didn't say anything, but disappeared into the bathroom.

We heard the shower come on almost before the door was closed.

"This house is so hectic," Jake said.

I told them I was going to bed. Coming out took way less time than I thought it would.

"Grant," Mom took my arm and pulled me over for a hug. She told me they were here for me, no matter what, and that they appreciated how I didn't expect them to immediately understand this news.

"Yeah, take as much time as you need," I said, looking at Dad. "I'm not going anywhere."

After that, I went to my room to chill, but Mom reminded me I needed to mop. And maybe it sounds stupid, but it did put me at ease a little that she treated me just like she did every other night.

School wasn't as bad as I thought it would be the next day. I got some weird looks and overheard people who were making up their own stories about my "wild and crazy" weekend, but I didn't care. I was determined to get through the rest of the semester and perform my best in all the football games we had coming up.

I still wanted to beat Skarzelli into a pulp, but football has taught me better sportsmanship than that. When I found out the coach was making him do an hour of extra exercises before every practice for the next month because of what he had done, I felt better. I still had to play with him and the other guys until the end of the season, but I knew it would be okay. They didn't really make fun of me afterwards anyway.

My parents have been pretty open with me about "the gay thing," asking me questions when they have them. Some of the questions I'd rather they Google search, so I don't answer all of them. But other than that, everything has been fine so far.

Before this ends, I'll tell you again that you're never alone, even when you feel like you are. There are always people you can talk to, even online, who can give you advice and help you figure things out about your sexuality if you have any questions.

Nothing is ever too hard that you can't handle it. I've built my whole life on football since I was little. It was my identity, and still is in a strong way. At first, I was totally humiliated when Skarz outed me like that in front of the guys, because it was so unexpected. However, I was nearly ready to come out on my own, so maybe it was a sign from the universe that it was the right time. I decided to make the best of it and start being openly unashamed.

I realized that having to explain that I like guys is just a little bump on the road to my goals of being a professional football player. I told myself, *a year from now, it won't matter.*

There have definitely been moments I've felt like no one understood. If you're feeling this way, let my story tell you that you aren't alone either, and that there are thousands of people with similar stories who know just what it feels like.

You are who you are, and this is your only life. You can do anything you set your mind to, and get past any obstacle.

I believe in you!

Author's Note

Thank you for reading this collection of coming out stories. I hope they kept touching your soul and you enjoyed reading them.

If you loved the book and have a minute to spare, I would really appreciate a short review on the Amazon site where you bought the book. Your help in spreading the word is greatly appreciated. Reviews from readers like you make a huge difference in helping new readers to find books like *Coming Out*.

And finally, one more thing. I love to get emails from people who have read my books, so please don't hesitate to drop me a line and share your thoughts about anything.

Thank you!
Jay Argent

jay@jayargent.com

Fairmont Boys Series from Jay Argent

Swimmer Boy (Book 1)

Liam Green is a sixteen-year-old boy who has just moved to Fairmont with his family. On his first day in his new high school, he falls for Alex, a handsome jock on the swim team. Alex doesn't seem to be gay, but that does not end Liam's obsession with him. Fate pushes the boys together, and they become friends—until Liam's secret is revealed.

Swimmer Boy begins a coming-of-age story about friendship and the kind of love that is found in the most unlikely places.

Other Books in Fairmont Boys series:

I am Not Gay (Book 2)
You Are Not My Son (Book 3)
The Death of the Good Guy (Book 4)
Best Friends Forever (Book 5)

Other Gay Themed Books from Jay

Operation Silent Moon

Corporal Dennis Benson is a Marine who serves in a special operations battalion together with Sergeant Adler Williams. Despite the tight bond between the elite unit Marines, Dennis has not found the courage to tell Adler, or the rest of his team, that he is gay. Adler's own life is turned upside down when his wife tells him that she is pregnant. Before the men can address their looming concerns, their worlds are shaken yet again.

Dennis and Adler are sent on a dangerous mission in South Sudan, where they meet Jafar, a young nurse who works at the US Embassy. Soon all three meet their enemies and their lives are in danger, unless they find a way to escape. Operation Silent Moon is a story about young men who are searching for their place in the big world.

About the Author

Jay Argent is a novelist in his forties who lives a peaceful life with his husband. His favorite hobbies are music, movies, and romantic novels. He obtained a degree in engineering in 2001 and built a successful career in a management consulting firm. Using his own high school and college experiences as inspiration, he is now pursuing his true passion of writing.

If you have any feedback, you can contact him by email at jay@jayargent.com. He very much looks forward to hearing from you.